FUJINO OMORI

ILLUSTRATION BY
KIYOTAKA HAIMURA

CHARACTER DESIGN BY
SUZUHITO YASUDA

AIZ WALLENSTEIN:
A Level 6 adventurer and Orario's
strongest swordswoman.

Is it WRONG
TO TRY TO
PICK UP GIRLS
IN A DUNGEON?
ON THE
SIDE

Sword Oratoria

© Kiyotaka Haimura

CONTENTS

PROLOGUE   ♦ A Moment of Water and Rest 001

CHAPTER 1   ♦ Passage and the Present 007

INTERLUDE   ♦ Flip Side of the Farce 029

CHAPTER 2   ♦ Rabbit Rookie 057

INTERLUDE   ♦ Flip Side of the Compromise 083

CHAPTER 3   ♦ 1/3 Pure Passion 105

INTERLUDE   ♦ Flip Side of the Stage 189

EPILOGUE   ♦ Homeward Bound 197

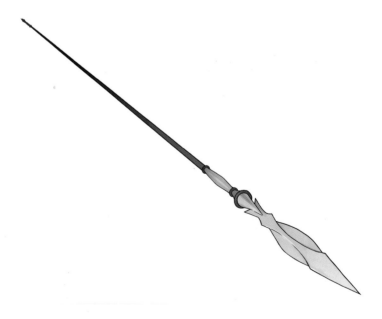

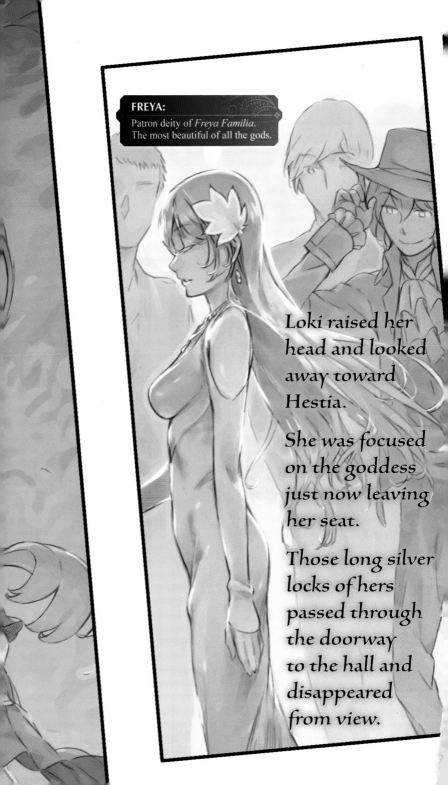

FREYA:
Patron deity of *Freya Familia*.
The most beautiful of all the gods.

Loki raised her head and looked away toward Hestia.

She was focused on the goddess just now leaving her seat.

Those long silver locks of hers passed through the doorway to the hall and disappeared from view.

"Those youngsters are certainly havin' a good time in spite of it all."

GARETH LANDROCK:
A veteran dwarf soldier and the oldest member of *Loki Familia*.

WELF CROZZO:
A young smith and a member of Bell's party. Human.

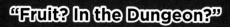

"Fruit? In the Dungeon?"

"Yes, this is fruit we collected here on the eighteenth floor."

"Mister Bell! Mister Bell! If you're not gonna eat that, Lilly wants it!"

The creature's great eye spun around and around before centering itself on Lefiya and Bell.

Sword Oratoria

IS it WRONG to TRY to PICK UP GIRLS iN A DUNGEON? ON THE SIDE

VOLUME 5

FUJINO OMORI

ILLUSTRATION BY
KIYOTAKA HAIMURA

CHARACTER DESIGN BY
SUZUHITO YASUDA

YEN
ON

NEW YORK

IS IT WRONG TO TRY TO PICK UP GIRLS IN A DUNGEON?
ON THE SIDE: SWORD ORATORIA, Volume 5
FUJINO OMORI

Translation by Liv Sommerlot
Cover art by Kiyotaka Haimura

DUNGEON NI DEAI WO MOTOMERU NO WA MACHIGATTEIRUDAROUKA GAIDEN
SWORD ORATORIA vol. 5
Copyright © 2015 Fujino Omori
Illustration copyright © Kiyotaka Haimura
Original Character Design © Suzuhito Yasuda
All rights reserved.
Original Japanese edition published in 2015 by SB Creative Corp.
This English edition is published by arrangement with SB Creative Corp., Tokyo, in care of Tuttle-Mori Agency, Inc., Tokyo.

English translation © 2018 by Yen Press, LLC

Yen On
1290 Avenue of the Americas
New York, NY 10104

Visit us at yenpress.com
facebook.com/yenpress
twitter.com/yenpress
yenpress.tumblr.com
instagram.com/yenpress

First Yen On Edition: February 2018

Yen On is an imprint of Yen Press, LLC.
The Yen On name and logo are trademarks of Yen Press, LLC.

Library of Congress Cataloging-in-Publication Data
Names: Ōmori, Fujino, author. | Haimura, Kiyotaka, 1973– illustrator. | Yasuda, Suzuhito, designer.
Title: Is it wrong to try to pick up girls in a dungeon? on the side: sword oratoria / story by Fujino Omori ; illustration by Kiyotaka Haimura ; original design by Suzuhito Yasuda.
Other titles: Danjon ni deai wo motomeru no wa machigatteirudarouka gaiden sword oratoria. English.
Description: New York, NY : Yen On, 2016– | Series: Is it wrong to try to pick up girls in a dungeon? on the side: sword oratoria
Identifiers: LCCN 2016023729 | ISBN 9780316315333 (v. 1 : pbk.) | ISBN 9780316318167 (v. 2 : pbk.) | ISBN 9780316318181 (v. 3 : pbk.) | ISBN 9780316318228 (v. 4 : pbk.) | ISBN 9780316442503 (v. 5 : pbk.)
Subjects: CYAC: Fantasy.
Classification: LCC PZ7.1.O54 Isg 2016 | DDC [Fic]—dc23
LC record available at https://lccn.loc.gov/2016023729

ISBNs: 978-0-316-44250-3 (paperback)
978-0-316-44251-0 (ebook)

1 3 5 7 9 10 8 6 4 2

LSC-C

Printed in the United States of America

VOLUME 5

FUJINO OMORI

ILLUSTRATION BY **KIYOTAKA HAIMURA**
CHARACTER DESIGN BY **SUZUHITO YASUDA**

A
Moment
OF
Water
AND
Rest

Гэта казка іншага сям'і.

Моманты вады і адпачынку

It feels good.

Aiz thought this to herself at the sensation of the water surrounding her.

"Ah......"

The breath escaping her lips felt distant. The sound of splashing water tickled her eardrums as the foam lapped at her skin and ears with soft, gentle caresses.

She was as naked as the day she was born.

Her eyes closed as water droplets drew rivulets down her smooth skin. They traced the curves of her breasts, down past her navel and slender stomach, before returning to the water's surface. Her beautiful golden hair was spread out like a fan, lilting to and fro in the water together with her glistening body.

She was gorgeous, her features rivaling even those of a goddess, and the sight of her lying where the water's surface met the air created a spectacle reminiscent of forest nymphs—mysterious and surreal. Had an artistically inclined individual been present to witness it, the scene would undoubtedly have been captured by brushstrokes.

It was a moment of pure bliss. She could actually feel the tension leaving her muscles as the pent-up fatigue racking her body melted away.

It was here and only here that she could forget everything, wrapped up in this protective world of water.

These thoughts trickled through her head as she let out another sigh that vibrated in her slender throat.

"...?"

All of a sudden.

Something blocked the white light shining on her closed eyelids, shrouding her face in darkness.

There was someone nearby, peering down at her—she could feel it in the ripples breaking against her skin.

She opened her eyes…revealing the pink-flushed cheeks of a certain elf maiden at point-blank range.

Lefiya…?

As the girl's name rose to Aiz's lips, the elf in question began appealing to her vehemently, her hand shielding her mouth and nose. Aiz, however, couldn't make out the words, her ears still beneath the water.

She was frantic now, and Aiz couldn't help but notice that Loki was right—the elf really was maturing. In fact, her bust behind the cover of her arm was almost the same size as Aiz's.

Aiz lowered her feet to the bath's floor and righted herself in the water.

"—have it all wrong, Miss Aiz! While I must admit the fantastical sight of you floating there in the water borders on the alluring, I…! I-I mean, were I artistically inclined, I would love to capture this scene in a painting to adorn my chambers, but I…! I-I mean I would never dream of sinking to the level of that lecherous goddess of ours! I-I merely noticed you over here and thought I would pay you a visit…!!" Lefiya was blushing hard as she sputtered out one excuse after another.

Though the young elf nearly idolized her, Aiz noticed none of it.

As the golden-haired girl cocked her head to the side curiously, a gleeful voice from off to the side drew her attention, and she turned.

Her eyes moved across the green leaves, countless trees, and blue crystals surrounding the wide pool she was currently occupying.

And in the middle of all that, she saw her companions—the other girls of *Loki Familia*—similarly disrobed and enjoying their time in the bath.

"Ha-*ha*! It feels amazing!!" Tiona squealed in delight as she pulled her head out from under a small waterfall dribbling down from a crack in the rocks. She proceeded to shake her drenched head, spraying water all over her nearby sister, who responded with an angry bark.

"What are you—a dog?! Stop that!!"

The two girls showed no modesty, baring to the world their robust tanned skin, slender waists, and ample chests. Their bodies had a different sort of elegance from Aiz's, but every celch of them was salaciously Amazonian.

"You're all so wonderfully...put together. Makes a girl shy," Leene mumbled to herself.

Next to her, Aki was busy washing the slender tail protruding from her backside. "You've got a plenty fine pair yourself there, Leene!" she replied with a twist of her hips.

"It's...it's only because I've put on some weight!" Leene's face reddened instantly. The girl's long hair, normally done up in braids, flowed down the length of her back as she brought both arms up to hide her chest.

Aki just shrugged. The velvet-haired, velvet-furred catgirl boasted very shapely breasts herself.

"Good gravy! Seems to me like *Loki Familia*'s a bunch of babes! Guess that's to be expected with a deity like yours, though, huh?" the half-dwarf woman, Tsubaki, mused aloud to herself as she meditated beneath the ten-meder-plus waterfall in the middle of the pool. Wiping her dark bangs away from her eye, she rose to her feet before heading toward the group, ever-present eye patch over her left eye.

Beads of water turned into tiny streamlets that worked their way across her olive skin, trickling enticingly down the nape of her neck and into the deep valley of her chest. Though normally restrained by a single sheet of cloth, her breasts were shapely enough to rival even Tione's.

The *Hephaistos Familia* smith let her eyes rove over the multiracial group of radiant women.

"Bet this'd be hard for the menfolk to resist. What would ya do if they came a-peekin', huh? Alicia? Narfi?" Tsubaki asked the two beautiful blondes, elf and human respectively.

"Punish them. And if their peeking just so happened to grant them an eyeful of Lady Riveria? They'd wish they'd never been born."

"Ah-ha-ha...I suppose you could say that even if they wanted to peek, they wouldn't have a chance."

The two second-tiers who had participated in the fifty-ninth-floor raid together with Aiz and the others fired a glance toward the pool's perimeter, where another set of female familia members stood vigilant with arrows and swords poised. The guards were fully prepared to administer an absolutely merciless whooping to anyone who dared trespass on these sacred grounds of femininity—monsters and men alike.

Thanks mostly to the fact that their patron deity was a female Casanova, there were decidedly more women than men in *Loki Familia*. Even including the leaders of the familia, a comparison of pure attack power undoubtedly favored the women's side.

This, in turn, led to feelings of inadequacy among the men of *Loki Familia*, surrounded as they were by this bevy of able-bodied women.

The elf and human pair waved appreciatively at their lookouts— they'd be trading places soon enough, and then it would be their turn to keep watch. The group of demi-humans responded with their own smiles.

The sight of so many young women stripped of their garments and armor was enough to make even the flowers blush.

It was moments like these that allowed them to let their hair down, even deep within the Dungeon's depths.

"Ahh, the eighteenth floor really is the best!" Tiona sighed leisurely as she floated on her back among the bluish glow of the surrounding forest. "Beautiful crystals and clear-blue water!"

Aiz couldn't help but mentally agree with the other girl.

While it was easy finding a place to wash in the Dungeon's various safety points—like the one on the fiftieth floor—it was just as easy to find a flowing pool or river to cleanse one's skin. That being said, this particular pool on the eighteenth floor was in a league of its own.

A brook of pure crystalline water cascaded down from deep within the floor's recesses. Cleaner and clearer than any river on the surface, it was an ideal spot for quenching thirst and soothing the bodies of humans and monsters alike. Even its name, the Under Resort, was in no way an overstatement.

"..."

Yes, this was the eighteenth floor.

Where Aiz and the others had stopped for a moment of respite after their incredible battle within the Dungeon's depths.

Their expedition to the unexplored frontier—the fifty-ninth floor—had come to an end, and it had been six days since they'd left their base camp on the fiftieth floor.

By all rights, they should have continued straight through to the surface, skipping this paradise entirely, so what were they doing there?

With the chattering of her peers and Lefiya's continued red-faced sputtering in her ears, Aiz turned her eyes up toward the giant, encompassing dome of the forest, letting her thoughts drift to the events that had led them there.

PASSAGE **AND**

THE PRESENT

Seven days prior, Aiz and the rest of the familia had descended to the fifty-ninth floor—the unexplored frontier—in an effort to increase their floor count.

What awaited them on that floor, however, was the unknown—a mutated floor of dense, junglelike trees and an abominable fiend called the "corrupted spirit."

It was a half-spirit, half-monster hybrid known as a demi-spirit.

Colossal in size and even capable of magic, it had attacked the party together with its legion of monsters, and upon its defeat, Aiz and the others had left immediately for their camp back on the fiftieth floor, where the remainder of their group awaited. Their rest there had been momentary at best, and soon they were on the move again, leaving behind the base camp.

The expedition party had hastily gotten ready to leave at Finn's prompt orders. The top-tier adventurers, exhausted as they were from their advance to the depths, had been shifted to the front, and the other familia members who'd been protecting the camp had been put in charge of all strenuous fighting en route. Not wanting to subject their bedraggled elites to any more unnecessary strain, they (along with Raul and the other supporters) had approached the task with gusto and given Aiz and the other top-tiers a chance to rest their weary bodies despite the long march ahead. And so they'd continued toward the surface, making good progress as they'd put floor after floor behind them.

However—

The Dungeon had not been so kind as to allow their triumphant return, nor did it ever when gallant adventurers headed back to the surface with their spoils of war after besting the bowels of its massive labyrinth.

"Was that a…scream?"

"You think someone's in trouble?"

They were on the lower floors when they heard it.

About halfway through their trek to the surface.

The long trail of people that made up their party was currently in the middle of a wide passageway. Aiz, Bete, and the other top-tiers at the front perked their ears up toward the back of the company, where, indeed, multiple screams could be heard.

"—Finn! Hasten the troops!"

The next shout came from the back of the line—the old soldier dwarf picking up the tail end of their formation. "We've got poison vermis on our hands here!" Gareth roared.

Almost instantaneously, they saw their companions making a mad rush toward them, followed by a swarm of maggot-like monsters.

Of all the poison-inflicting monsters in the Dungeon, poison vermis were the most dangerous. The toxin they spewed from their mouths and secreted from their pores was powerful enough to afflict even upper-class adventurers, who had strong status resistances. Though their attack power itself was decidedly low, the small beasts had a tendency to spring forth from carcasses in droves, much like actual maggots, garnering them the nickname "poison graveyards."

This time was no exception. In fact, the teeming throng making a beeline for *Loki Familia* was so dense with wriggling maggots, not even Aiz and the other top-tiers could believe their eyes.

"S-so many! Is it a mass spawn?!"

"At a time like this…?! We're in trouble!"

Mass spawns were just another one of the Dungeon's Irregulars.

As everyone in the party ran while supporting those among them unable to fight, the stampeding mass of more than a hundred poisonous maggot monsters crawled, writhed, and scrambled its way toward them, covering the walls and ceiling like a larval invasion. Aiz and the others swallowed their feelings of revulsion and immediately rushed to their companions' aid.

Aiz with her Airiel and Bete with his Airiel-infused Frosvirt joined Gareth and his giant shield to stave off the incoming poisonous spray while Tiona and Tione hurriedly dragged anyone suffering from purple lesions back to safety. Riveria attempted to seal off the tunnel with her freezing magic, but the vermis simply went around. More and more of them were squirming out of countless side passages before regrouping, just as strong.

"Th-there's no end to them!" Lefiya's face paled at the sight as she began Concurrent Casting from within the party's center.

It was a monster party—a floor-wide bout of continuous spawning as opposed to a single large-scale spawn. And what's more, the monster involved was the poison vermis, known for its tendency to move in swarms, which only exacerbated the situation.

Loki Familia's adventurers had already exhausted their supplies and their strength, both physical and mental, every reserve, during their demanding expedition. This random encounter was hard to bear. Even the flames of the few magic swords they had remaining were too little, too late.

Aiz and the other top-tiers wasted no time transitioning from the offensive to withdrawal once their companions were safe.

"Finn! We're losin' 'em! Rakuta and the others need help right now!!"

"Captain, do you think we should head back to the safety point…?"

Tiona and Tione called respectively, carting a boy-girl pair of hume bunnies who were currently groaning in pain.

"We don't know the scope of this Irregular! If poison vermis are spawning on the lower floors, too, we'll be trapped there!" Finn shouted back in between spear thrusts at the front of the party, brushing aside their comments. "Even if we did manage to hole ourselves up there, the time it would take launching a counteroffensive would leave us no chance to heal the injured properly!" he added as he took out a particularly large monster blocking their path.

To make matters worse, they didn't have a single antidote left.

"We'll head to the eighteenth floor! Everyone, double-time! Carry those who can't walk if you have to!"

Lefiya and the others complied with the captain's orders without a second thought.

Grabbing the legs and arms of their fellow familia members who'd fallen prey to the poison, they took off at a full sprint. Meanwhile, Aiz and the other top-tiers positioned themselves to the rear, center, and front of the disorganized formation, doing their best to support their companions on the march.

Giant maggots—easily more than thirty celches—oozed their deadly discharge as they dropped on the fleeing party from the ceiling like purple rain. Even the accompanying *Hephaistos Familia* smiths were screaming now.

"This is borderin' on madness! Even the other beasties are gettin' caught up in it!" Tsubaki bisected a whole swath of incoming poison vermis as she watched a nearby monster writhe in poison-induced pain.

The screams of humans and monsters alike filled the passageway as *Loki Familia* carried and dragged their wounded toward the stairs, charging their way onto the eighteenth floor.

"Didn't wanna let us go quietly, I see." Finn sighed in spite of himself.

They had set up within the forest at the southern corner of the eighteenth floor—the safety zone—quite near to the tunnel that would take them up to the seventeenth. Finn and the others had quickly set the rest of the familia to work establishing a new base camp.

The injured adventurers and smiths were splayed out in the grass beneath the trees or inside their tents with the flaps pulled back so the breeze could pass through. Men, women, humans, demi-humans—every victim was covered in a cold sweat, purple lesions dotting their skin.

Guttural moans of agony permeated the air.

Finn, Riveria, and Gareth looked out over the sordid scene from their spot beside the main tent.

"Everyone with lower than a G in resistance has been immobilized... Even the high smiths have been downed—everyone besides Tsubaki, that is. As expected, that poison is no joke."

"The Dungeon is an unforgivin' mistress, after all…Hoped she'd go easy on us this time."

Riveria's and Gareth's words were heavy as they conversed, no doubt the decisive battle in the unexplored frontier still weighing on their minds.

This poison-vermis attack had further rubbed salt in their wounds.

Nearly all the lower-level members, supporters included, had succumbed to vermis poisoning. With more than a third of the entire expedition affected, they wouldn't be leaving there anytime soon.

Finn and the others had no choice but to settle everyone in for a large-scale rest.

"Riveria, how goes the healing?" Finn asked.

"We're prioritizing those with the heaviest injuries, but…I do hope you're not expecting too much. Detoxification magic is rare, and we have only a few mages and healers capable of casting it—myself included." Riveria lowered her eyes to her Mind-fatigued body. She could feel her power returning bit by bit thanks to her Regen ability, but it was still far from adequate, and she closed her eyes with regret. "What's more, even with antidotal magic, poison-vermis venom is difficult to treat. I can't promise full recoveries."

The toxin of the poison vermis required a very particular treatment—made from its own secretions—and without it, complete recovery was impossible.

Normal detox magic simply wouldn't cut it. Even those with the highest levels of magic power couldn't hope to do more than weaken the effects of the poison. The only person Finn knew with healing magic advanced enough to completely cure the affliction was Amid Tessanare, "Dea Saint," of *Dian Cecht Familia*.

"We'll need the antidote if we're to have any hope of healing everyone."

"Yes. We'll have to wait for Bete, after all."

While everyone had rushed to set up camp and care for the injured the night before—or at least during what passed for "night" within the Dungeon—Finn had instructed Bete to continue on to the surface and purchase the antivenin from one of the stores in Orario.

Bete was easily the fastest runner in the familia. Skill effects included, his speed surpassed even that of Finn and every other higher-level adventurer in *Loki Familia* (though just barely). While he still couldn't compare to Aiz when she activated Airiel, what with the distance involved and the battle-weary condition of the party as a whole, someone with reliable swiftness and endurance was necessary, making Bete the perfect one for the task.

"You always give me the grunt work!" the werewolf had grumbled before taking off into the night.

No doubt, he had already reached the surface, hurriedly collecting enough doses of the rare, expensive antidote to cure the whole party. Finn estimated Bete would be back in two days' time.

Though the afflicted would have to suffer for those two days, so long as Riveria and the other mages continued their detox treatments, it wasn't likely anyone's condition would deteriorate further.

"First the Durandal from Tsubaki, then the thirty-some magic swords, and now a mother lode of antivenin...Gotta give all the drops to those smiths, too! We're really gonna be in the red this time!"

"I ask that you not think of that now, Gareth," Finn pleaded with a wry smile. "You'll give me a headache."

On top of their unforeseen expenditures, they still had to relinquish most of the drop items from the Dungeon's depths to *Hephaistos Familia* as per their initial agreement. This included the valgang-dragon fangs and scales they'd risked their lives for, as well as everything they'd picked up from the fifty-second floor on down.

Though their efforts had rewarded them with an increased floor count, all they'd earned toward paying off the massive costs of their expedition was a few magic stones—to say they were in a bind was an understatement. If it weren't for the reward Aiz had received from her quest in the twenty-fourth floor's pantry, their outlook would have been even bleaker.

"Perhaps profits should be top priority on our next expedition... whenever that is," Finn muttered to himself. "...I wanted to inform Loki of the events on the fifty-ninth floor as quickly as possible, but it seems circumstances aren't on my side. For now, I've simply written everything in a letter. I'll have to trust that Bete will deliver it." Raising his head toward the ceiling, he narrowed his eyes against the speckled light peeking in from among the forest's branches. "I suppose fretting will lead us nowhere. If we take the optimistic view, it has given us an excuse to spend some time on the eighteenth floor, right?" His voice was airy, tinged with mirth, as he turned around and let his eyes wander.

Finn's words elicited mildly chagrined smiles from Riveria and Gareth, and as he continued to survey the camp, he noticed Raul and some other men of the familia, currently the only ones at work guarding the perimeter and caring for the sick. Finn had sent Aiz and the rest of the female squadron to the forest pool for a soak in hopes of relieving the pent-up exhaustion and gloom. He had plans to send the men there, too, once the ladies returned.

"Ye sure ye didn't want to go with Aiz and the others, Riveria? Coulda left it to us to watch over things for a spell."

"My presence would only make the other elves hypersensitive. I wouldn't be able to properly relax," the high elf responded, and it was true—the other elves would turn instantly into courtesans guarding their queen if Riveria were to join them, making it difficult for her to really indulge in the bath's pleasures. "I'm fine being the last one," she finished with a small smile.

"While we mustn't throw caution to the wind, we are well past the climax of our expedition. Perhaps we should try to get some rest, too?" Finn posed.

Riveria and Gareth had no objections to the tiny captain's suggestion, nodding in agreement as fatigue tugged at their bodies.

"Fall baaaaack! It's the men's turn!"

"All right! Finally our time to wash up..."

"Once again, not a single opportunity for a peep or two of the girls..."

"You idiot! That place is like a holy sanctuary, divine protection and all. And even if it wasn't, there are still plenty of reasons to keep our distance."

"Yeah, like an appreciation for our lives."

"Stop it already, guys. Let's just go!...If Aki and the others hear any of this, I'll be in huge trouble..." Raul urged his companions, attempting to keep the other *Loki Familia* men in line as he led them toward the forest pool for their own round of bathing and accompanying guard duty.

Moans and groans continued to pervade the base camp. While color had started returning to many of the victims' faces, most were still bedridden and far from total recovery. Aiz and Lefiya were tasked with lookout duty while support healers like Leene earnestly tended to the sick adventurers and smiths.

"Pretty much what we expected, I guess. Rivira's nothin' but a massive rip-off!"

"Taking advantage of people in need. It's enough to make me livid."

"Welcome back, Miss Tiona, Miss Tione," Lefiya greeted the two Amazons upon their return to camp. The twins were on their way back from a short shopping trip in the town of Rivira on the western edge of the floor.

The Dungeon town had actually been their first stop when they'd arrived on the eighteenth floor. What with the lower-level adventurers in critical condition, they'd needed to buy up every vial of poison-vermis antivenin they could find, even if it meant paying the astronomical prices charged by vendors in the aptly named "Rogue Town." Managed by upper-class adventurers, the shops of Rivira charged an arm and a leg for their goods, well over what those same items would cost on the surface. Tiona and Tione had gone to visit the town again in an attempt to barter for some basic foodstuffs, but as they described in some detail upon their arrival back at camp, they had found nothing but exorbitant prices. Those prices were the very reason *Loki Familia* set up a camp of their own rather than take advantage of the relay town's services.

The merchants there, in striking contrast to the beautiful crystalline landscape surrounding the settlement, had been just as ill-mannered and overbearing as always.

"We managed to scrape together enough magic stones and drops on the way there to trade for a bit of bread, but…it ain't gonna last. Not when our supplies are practically gone already," Tiona commented.

"It'll still be a while before Bete comes back…Guess we don't have a choice but to gather supplies on this floor after all," Tione responded.

"Ah! Do you mean fruit from the forest?" Lefiya made a guess, and Tione confirmed it while her sister rubbed her exposed belly next to her.

"We need to watch our expenses right now, but we can't expect everyone to just go hungry," she added, shoulders drooping.

Which meant they'd need to be self-sufficient—exactly how adventurers were originally.

"Let's get word to Aki and the others to put together some small teams. We can collect water, then head to the forest and gather whatever food we can find," Tione suggested, to which Aiz, Lefiya, and Tiona nodded in agreement.

"Got it."

"Understood!"

"Let's do it!"

The bathing pool wasn't the only source of water in the forest on the eighteenth floor—there were also small freshwater creeks running across the landscape—and produce from the fruit trees scattered among the vegetation was edible to both monsters and people alike.

Tione ended up organizing the women into groups of twos and threes, making sure each group had at least one Level 3 or higher. While no monsters spawned within the boundaries of the safety point itself, there would still be numerous beasts that had traveled there from different floors to contend with, and the large forest or the wetlands to the north were sure to be home to at least a few monsters.

Tione strongly encouraged the groups to be cautious during their search.

"Shall we get going, then?"

"Yes! Let's do our best, Miss Aiz!" Lefiya answered.

The two of them had been tasked with collecting food. As the different groups set off from the camp, they, too, made their way into the dense thicket of trees.

The dim light of the crystals growing from the Dungeon's ceiling peeked between the gaps in the canopy overhead, tingeing the world around them in hazy, piebald patterns as bluish crystal stalagmites rose from the bases of the trees.

They split up the duties as they went, Lefiya gathering fruits to add to her pouch as Aiz surveyed the perimeter for signs of danger.

A lone bugbear monster decided to attack them at one point, but Aiz finished it off with a single swing of her Durandal weapon, Desperate. Even after the long expedition, the silver sword remained in pristine condition. The honing Tsubaki had given it didn't hurt, either. The sword's blade now boasted a healthy, razor-like sharpness.

As Aiz watched the monster turn to ash beneath her sword, Lefiya's hand roamed from tree to tree in search of fruit. Her fingers curled around a tuft of Honey Cloud—a cotton-like fruit seemingly infused in honey. The sickly sweet smell of the juices dripping from its skin made her mouth water, but she forced herself to pack it away in her pouch with a determined shake of her head.

Just like the self-repairing labyrinth walls, these trees were also a component of the Dungeon and would bear new fruit after a certain period of time. In addition to the Honey Cloud, Lefiya was able to gather some squash-shaped gourd berries, among other things. The abundance of fruit made it feel like an orchard, and she told herself to commit the area to memory as she glanced around at the rich harvest.

Aiz continued to monitor their surroundings near the elf, but after a long while without any incident, she, too, began packing fruits away in her pouch.

"Ah…a crystal drop."

"Oh my! Those are so rare, Miss Aiz! That's truly amazing!"

They were on their way back to the base camp with considerably heavier pouches, when Aiz discovered a pale-blue sparkle in the grasses at her feet. The tear-shaped, candy-like fruit was hidden among the tiny clumps of crystal that could be found covering the ground in every direction.

The rare item—or perhaps "rare fruit" would be more accurate—was none other than a crystal drop, and to find one was quite exceptional, even here on the eighteenth floor.

"If you tried to buy this on the surface, it would be very expensive! It's often known as the 'Nobleman's Candy'…I have only tried it once, myself, but I couldn't agree more with the name. Pleasantly crisp with a wonderfully refined flavor. Quite delicious, really!"

Exactly as Lefiya excitedly described, the hard-candy-like crystal drop was not only delicious but a rare delicacy. Its jewel-like beauty had made it popular among the city's elite as a high-class confection, and a jar of them could go for well over ten thousand on the surface.

Though they had found only two, the sight of the drops atop Aiz's palm made Lefiya's eyes glimmer.

As Aiz watched her sweets-craving junior eye the two candies, a sudden idea popped into her mind, and her lips curled into an ever-so-discreet smile.

Without hesitation, she placed the crystal drops in the elf's hand.

"Miss Aiz, what are you…?"

"I'm giving them…to you."

"B-but you were the one to find them, Miss Aiz! And they're quite valuable!"

Aiz's smile returned as she watched Lefiya frantically sputtering, her staff in her left hand and the candies in her right.

"It's…a thank-you."

"Thank-you?"

Aiz responded with a nod. "For saving me...on the fifty-ninth floor."

Lefiya's azure eyes popped open in surprise.

On the fifty-ninth floor, they'd faced off against that demi-spirit. Aiz had leaped toward that mighty creature only to fall straight into a trap, with mere moments before she would be shot out of the sky.

It was then that Lefiya's magic had saved her.

The spell of the elf, who'd refused to give up despite countless injuries, had flown straight and true, protecting Aiz from the enemy's attack.

"What with everything that's happened, I haven't really had a chance to say it yet, so...thank you, Lefiya. Thank you for saving me."

The faintest of blushes tingeing her cheeks, Aiz's face broke into a smile.

And as Lefiya looked into the eyes of the golden-haired, golden-eyed swordswoman, as she heard her pure, unadulterated gratitude, her own eyes became unexpectedly wet.

She brought an arm up instantly to wipe at her face, growing more and more flushed as her actions grew more and more questionable.

"It's—Y-you mustn't say things like that, Miss Aiz! It is I who should be grateful! You and the others have saved me so, so many times, and...and this was merely my chance to return the favor...!"

"No...it's fine that way. I said it before, too...right?"

They would protect her as many times as they had to.

And Lefiya would use her magic to save them.

That was what Aiz had told her many days ago. And as the words drifted back into her memory, Lefiya felt her movements come to a halt. Then the smallest yet most triumphant sort of smile spread across her face.

Abashment still coloring her features, she turned her eyes downward to stare at the two crystal drops in her hand.

"Thank you..." she finally uttered as she carefully placed the two bluish-white sparkles, her medal for saving Aiz, into the inner breast pocket of her battle clothes.

"Even Tiona and Tione said you were amazing. If you weren't there, who knows what could've happened."

"It—it was all thanks to Miss Filvis...! Oh, but of course your and Lady Riveria's tutelage, as well, I...I, erm..."

"Finn was happy, too. That we...that you had grown so strong." Aiz's deluge of praise continued.

"Th-the captain?! I-I mean...that's...o-oh my..." The excessive compliments from the girl she'd admired for so long finally became too much, and Lefiya's face turned a brilliant shade of red. Unable to bear it any further, she lowered her eyes, both hands tightly gripped around her staff, radiating heat up to the tips of her pointed ears.

The scene made Aiz smile all the more, and the swordswoman thought to herself how truly amazing Lefiya had been.

The girl in front of her had grown so much between this expedition and the last that she was scarcely recognizable.

Every spell Lefiya had woven in those many battles had helped shape her into the mage she was today.

Aiz found herself wondering what it was that had spurred her on, pushing her to achieve results. As she stood there looking at the younger girl, Lefiya slowly raised her head.

"Um...Miss Aiz?"

"?"

"The boy the captain mentioned back on the fifty-ninth floor... Bell Cranell?" There wasn't a hint of unrest in Lefiya's voice as she spoke, her eyes as sharp as tacks, and Aiz felt her heart jump in her chest.

It had been during Braver's encouraging speech in the midst of that decisive battle down on the fifty-ninth floor. The magic-like courage he'd used to turn the tides of the battle, reversing everything even as an overwhelming despair had gripped their hearts.

It was then that he'd brought up the name of that boy, Bell Cranell.

"Did that human adventurer...do something as we were making our way to the fifty-ninth floor?"

Back when Aiz had been giving her training for Concurrent Casting in preparation for the expedition, Lefiya had finally been unable to take it any longer and asked for the name of Aiz's other mentee, and the swordswoman had replied with that boy's name. However, Lefiya hadn't known about what had transpired down on the ninth floor—his ferocious battle with the minotaur.

Upon hearing that a minotaur had spawned on the upper levels, Finn and the other top-tier adventurers had broken away from the vanguard temporarily to appraise and handle the situation. This much Lefiya had heard from Raul and her fellow familia members. However, the details as to exactly what Aiz and the others had witnessed at the scene remained undisclosed.

When Finn had mentioned him, it had set off something and changed everything.

Hearing that boy's name had lit a fire within Aiz's heart, within Bete's—within everyone's.

Even Lefiya had been able to tell instinctively that something had happened.

As the elf's azure eyes stared through her, Aiz's gaze traveled up toward the speckled canvas of trees hanging over their heads, almost as though she was searching for something.

"Mm-hm…He had his own adventure."

The array of crystals visible through the leaves spread out across the ceiling like chrysanthemums, guiding her line of sight farther upward toward the floors above.

"He was truly amazing…just like you, Lefiya." The words slipped from her mouth so easily, betraying her true feelings.

Lefiya's grip around her staff tightened with a jerk.

That boy…changed, too.

Aiz lost herself in her thoughts, unaware of Lefiya's current turmoil.

Compared to Lefiya—there was no doubt that whatever the boy's adventure had been like, it could never top the elf's achievements.

But his adventure symbolized the starting point for Aiz and the other adventurers.

The weak defeating the impossibly strong-armed, relying on nothing but their own strength.

It was one of the simplest yet most difficult feats of all.

And Aiz and the others had been completely taken by it—the idea of betting everything for a chance to overcome one's limits.

One's first successful exploit would have a major influence on one's life.

Everybody's first adventure simply held that much meaning.

There was no question that the boy would continue to grow and change from here on out. Aiz was sure of it.

Would he succeed? Would it merely make him reckless? Or would he become something else entirely?

Maybe he'd use his newly acquired qualification for herohood to begin scaling that far-off, impregnable peak?

—*What is he doing right now?*

"..."

Aiz narrowed her eyes against the sight of those pure white crystals blooming on the ceiling.

The elf, too, followed her gaze, the two of them simply drinking in their ivory radiance.

"Night" had fallen across the eighteenth floor.

When the white clump of crystals at the center of the mass of blue glowed like the sun, the crystalline ceiling made them feel as if the sky from the surface was rolled out above their heads.

As time passed, however, the artificial light dimmed, bathing the floor in shadow and simulating a familiar twilight.

Once Aiz and the others had returned from their bout of scavenging, all of *Loki Familia* settled down for dinner within the circle of guards standing watch and portable magic-stone lanterns.

They feasted on the fruits Aiz and the others had harvested, as well as what little bread Tiona and Tione had managed to purchase in Rivira. Tsubaki had brought back some mushrooms from the nearby Wooden Labyrinth as well, and they grilled them whole over the campfire.

The half-dwarf had taken full advantage of her position as a guest in the group. Traveling about wherever she pleased—though she did make sure someone was taking care of her smiths in her stead—she'd first gone off monster hunting and then used the spoils to trade for alcohol and other various necessities in Rivira. Even with the alliance between their two familias, her actions should not be condoned, but given that the expedition was already over, Finn and the other elites simply let it slide with wry smiles of amusement.

Of course, such behavior was strictly prohibited for anyone from their own familia.

"M-Miss Tsubaki, are you sure these mushrooms are edible...?" Raul raised the question as a bead of sweat dribbled down his forehead. "We haven't even checked if they're suitable for human consumption...!"

"Aw, come on! As long as you've got a status with decent resistance, you'll be fiiiiine!" Tsubaki was currently toasting the large purple mushrooms over open flames, sending up a considerable amount of embers in her mildly intoxicated state.

"So they are poisonous?!"

"Aww, don't be like that! They're a rare delicacy, seriously! C'mon, you try one, Thousand Elf!"

"I-I must respectfully decline!" Lefiya responded with a frightened shout.

"Oh man! Let me eat one!"

Tiona enthusiastically reached toward the mushrooms everyone else was emphatically refusing, prompting a laugh from the others. Even Aiz felt a smile form on her lips.

As soon as the boisterous dinner came to an end, the group retired for the night.

Guard duty was to be handled in shifts, though Aiz and the other elites were, of course, exempt. At that moment, Tiona, Tione, Lefiya, and the other female members were sound asleep together in the tent they had been given since all other accommodations were being used to house the injured.

Sensing that the second-tier elf had left for her own night-watch shift, Aiz focused on recovering her strength.

Before she knew it, it was "morning."

"…"

Light had returned to the eighteenth floor of the Dungeon, and a hazy forest sunrise settled over the camp as Aiz emerged from the tent.

She was wide awake.

She always was when traveling deep within the Dungeon.

A truly sound sleep was impossible within this underground labyrinth, no matter how tired someone happened to be.

Big time difference between the surface and down here…

The crystals on the eighteenth floor dimmed and brightened according to their own schedule, creating a gap between the day cycle of the surface and that of the Dungeon, which often discomfited visiting adventurers.

Lefiya's small pocket watch sitting next to her pillow indicated that it was only a few hours past midnight, meaning that the world aboveground was still blanketed in darkness underneath the light of the moon.

As Aiz stared up at the heavenly rock formations hanging overhead, she found herself craving the light of the sun, the peaceful tranquility of the moon—she'd seen neither for nearly two weeks now.

Fastening her trusted sword, Desperate, to her side, she notified the others of her departure and left camp behind her for a brief walk. She was up anyway, and it would feel good to stretch her legs. She might even do a bit of sword training—something she'd had little chance to do since delving into the Dungeon.

All these thoughts were drifting across her mind as her boots swished through the grasses, when suddenly—

"_____—*oooooaaaaaarrrrr!*"

"!"

—the far-off howl of something massive reached her, almost like a rumble in the ground.

A colossal *boooom* immediately followed, causing the earth to tremble.

Her top-tier-adventurer senses tingling, Aiz knew at once that something was wrong. The floor boss, Goliath, was on the move in the large hall above her on the seventeenth floor.

Aiz took off.

This was the first she'd heard of the beast since they had set up camp. Which had to mean that the seventeenth floor's Monster Rex had just recently spawned and was now attacking an adventurer who'd trespassed on its domain. The fact that she could feel the vibrations so strongly, too, was a sign that the brute's iron hammer was wreaking havoc in the passage connecting the two floors.

Loki Familia's camp was at the floor's southern tip, close to the cave leading to the seventeenth floor.

Concerned for the safety of her companions, Aiz hurtled toward the floor entrance.

Sprinting through the trees, leaping over the knolls of crystal, she flew out of the dim exit to the forest.

And then.

...Huh?

She saw a group of adventurers sprawled out on the ground.

They were lying on a bed of green grass just outside the cave's entrance.

There were three—two male humans and a prum female.

It was a horrible sight. The unconscious prum girl's face was littered with scratches and covered in dust, while the red-haired human boy passed out next to her appeared to have broken his left leg, judging from its ghastly angle. It seemed as if they had rushed to this floor in a last-ditch attempt to escape.

However, it was the last boy whom Aiz couldn't stop looking at.

Dust and sand discolored his snow-white hair.

His lightweight equipment was scratched, and the salamander-wool linens inside were shredded.

He was facedown in the grass, unmoving.

Blood poured freely from his forehead, staining what she could see of his face a dark crimson.

—*It can't be.*

Aiz's mind went blank for a moment, her feet glued to the ground, before she managed to start moving forward in a half daze.

She was having trouble thinking, and the sounds around her seemed so, so far away. It felt as if she were traveling through a white tunnel—her thoughts, her vision, everything was obscured by a pale shroud from the sheer terror and shock of the sight in front of her.

Rustle, rustle, went her feet through the grass as she neared the prone boy.

She stopped in front of him, gazing downward as her shadow veiled the boy's slender frame.

He was breathing—that much she could tell for sure—but then…

…his hand twitched.

"!!"

Suddenly, he gripped her left foot.

Aiz couldn't help but wince when his trembling fingers dug into her boot as his bloodied face slowly rose up toward her.

Then his lips parted, using what seemed like every ounce of strength he had left.

"Please…save my…friends…!" he pleaded hoarsely.

As though fearing she might not understand, he turned his clouded rubellite eyes toward the two adventurers on the ground next to him. Then, his hand slackened, and completely spent, he lost consciousness.

Aiz found her bearings, dropping to her knees and running her fingers over the boy's bloodstained bangs and forehead.

"Bell…?"

But the boy's face remained motionless.

It hadn't even been two weeks since his grand adventure—his fight with that minotaur.

Now, at this mid-level Dungeon paradise where nature and crystal lived in harmony, Aiz and Bell were together again for a reunion that no one could have seen coming.

INTERLUDE

Flip Side of the Farce

Гэта казка іншага сям'і.

Задняя бок камедыі

Let's rewind a bit to a day long before Aiz and company arrived at the safety point on the eighteenth floor. To a point only four days into *Loki Familia's* expedition, when a certain meeting was about to take place.

"Yahooo! It's Denatus time!!"

The shout came from Babel, the soaring white tower in the center of Orario.

Gods aplenty had gathered in the great hall on the tower's thirtieth floor.

It was time for Denatus, the grand meeting of the deities that took place once every three months.

Denatus was a gathering that was mostly bluster and didn't accomplish much. That being said, it was an advisory body technically recognized by the Guild. Discussions at these events were dominated by inane topics of little to no consequence—truly representative of the gods' capricious natures—but every once in a while, more important matters were brought up: the bequeathment of influential aliases onto adventurers, for instance, or the proposal and subsequent evaluation of potential events and festivities. Accordingly, there were times they had to convene outside the normal schedule.

The only requirement for participation in a Denatus was at least one upper-class adventurer within the god's familia—in other words, at least one member needed to be Level 2 or higher. Pitting their familias against one another and comparing the ability of their followers to level up—to transcend the limitations of their current status—was just another way for the gods to jostle for status on the mortal plane.

Because an adventurer's level was synonymous with how closely they stood to the gods themselves, the number of high-level followers in one's familia had become a sort of achievement, a way to be recognized by their peers, as it were.

"Whoa! Even Lady Freya's here?!"

"Hell yeaaaaaaaaaaaaaaaaaaah!!"

"And Lady Ishtar, too!"

"Ain't she a sight for sore eyes...!"

The large room was one giant circular hall, countless long pillars supporting a ceiling far overhead. The blue sky beyond the thirtieth-floor windows surrounded them on all sides, imparting the feeling that the guests were traversing a holy temple in the clouds. Deities appeared one after another from the giant door that acted as the room's sole exit, and the line made its way toward the massive round table in the center of the room.

There was a double-bunned god radiating austerity, an elephant-faced god emphatically introducing himself every chance he could get ("I am Ganeeesha!"), and a pair of silver- and purple-haired goddesses of beauty—these latter two garnered quite a lot of attention from the men. This, in turn, prompted more than a few eye rolls from the women. Old gods, young gods, male and female alike, all took their seats around the giant round table.

The room was filled with smiles as deities took the opportunity to chat among their neighbors.

After a short while, one of the goddesses rose to her feet.

"Well! We're all here, ain't we? Let's get this show on the road!" Loki's crimson hair gave a bounce as her narrow eyes squinted into a smile of their own. The room grew quiet, and she continued. "Let the one thousand something-th meeting of the gods, Denatus, commence! I'll be yer host, Loki! Pleasure to be here tonight."

"Woooooo!"

The gathering of exuberant gods burst into applause.

Loki responded to the ovation of her peers with an energetic raise of her arm.

The trickster goddess's organizing of the month's Denatus hadn't been an accident. No, Loki herself had asked to be the host.

"Most of my kids are out on their expedition, leavin' me with nothin' to do! What say you guys let me host this month's Denatus, huh?"

That had been her proposition.

Keeping the group of loquacious, unmanageable gods under control required a god of considerable rank. As the patron deity of one of the largest familias in Orario, Loki had been met with nothing but encouraging replies of "*Be our guest!*" in response to her offer.

Loki looked out across the table of gods and goddesses. There were, of course, many familiar faces, from the goddess of beauty Freya—with whom she maintained a trying yet inescapable relationship—to the scarlet-haired, scarlet-eyed goddess Hephaistos—with whom she was currently allied. The latter beamed a smile at Loki in greeting, her right eye covered by its ever-present eye patch.

In the process of surveying the table, she couldn't help but notice the young goddess sitting beside the deity of the forge.

Ugh, so Itty-Bitty really did come? Cheeky little thing...

The short-statured girl gave a shudder as their eyes met. Her jet-black hair was done up in twin pigtails by a set of bell-shaped fasteners, and the overwhelming presence of her massive chest was almost paralyzing.

The sight of that detestable Loli-goddess and her eyesore of a bosom made Loki want to violently lose her lunch. It was none other than the pint-size busty Jyaga Maru tramp—Loki's rival in all things breast related.

She simply glared back at Loki, "*You got a problem, huh?*" written all over her face.

Under normal circumstances, the two would have begun quarreling the moment they'd laid eyes upon each other.

Ah, whatever. Who gives a damn about her anyway? I've got things to do!

Loki decided to ignore her.

The fact that the red-haired goddess didn't lunge at her from that single look was enough to arouse suspicion in the buxom girl, but Loki didn't let it faze her, carrying on with her hosting duties in blithe ignorance.

"All right, then! Let's get on with it, shall we? We'll start with a little information swap. Anyone got any juicy tidbits they'd like to share?"

"I do, I do! I've heard tell that old Soma got a slap on the wrist from the Guild and had all his precious liquor confiscated!"

"He *whaaaaaaaaaaaaaaaaaaaaaaaaaa*?!"

Loki's question was like a spark, and soon the whole hall was abuzz.

The main goal of Denatus was the sharing of information. Most tidbits ended up being nothing but frivolous gossip merely meant to relieve some boredom, but on the off chance someone had news relating to Orario or the Dungeon, they'd identify it as a point of discussion and share it appropriately.

Denatus was a meeting of the most influential gods and goddesses of Orario, and those same gods had a duty to relay any- and everything of note.

This often resulted in a wild affair.

Gods raised their hands left and right, spouting off their opinions in a sort of mass chaos akin to a congressional parliament. One topic led to another, which led to yet another, and conversations were always in a constant state of flux and laced with riotous laughter.

The "solemn assembly of the gods" many mortals envisioned when they imagined the Denatus was, in fact, nothing of the sort. If they had a chance to see what the event was really like, most would probably say, "So our gods act exactly the same as always…"

"All right, everyone quiet for a sec!"

Loki's shout instantly silenced the cacophony of voices all trying to prove their points.

"Lessee now. Lookin' at everything that's been brought up, it seems the matter we need to address the most is the whole Rakia shebang. For the time bein', we'll relay what we know to the Guild. Having said that, I highly doubt ol' Ouranos isn't aware. But anyway, as some of ya here've probably already called your familias together, could one of ya take care of it?"

"*Got it!*"

Loki exercised her authority as chair to deal with the topic promptly and concisely.

The other gods nodded in obedient agreement.

"Ah, right. 'S it okay if I throw one more issue of my own into the pot?" Loki cut in with a little grin once it seemed the other gods had run out of topics and there was a lull in the conversation.

She ran her eyes around the entirety of the table, letting them fall conspicuously on two certain male gods sitting a short distance away from each other.

The two gods—the golden-haired Dionysus and the gentlemanly Hermes—squinted with identical little smiles in response.

"Recently, a nasty *new monster species* has been comin' out of the woodwork. We saw 'em at 'Philia and now they're even showin' up at safety points."

There was a simultaneous flinch from a number of the gods.

The stunning silver-locked goddess of beauty threw Loki a side-long glance as the young, buxom goddess next to Hephaistos cocked her head to the side in oblivious curiosity.

Several deities, whose familias earned a living in the Dungeon or sent many of their adventurers to Rivira, were wearing very stiff expressions on their usually graceful features—perhaps they knew something? Or some of their followers had already become victims of those creatures?

"These vibrant little beasties look like someone went at 'em with a paintbrush. They're 'bout as strong as a second-tier adventurer… and damn elusive, too. They have a tendency to show up wherever they goddamn well please, whether it's in the Dungeon or *even the city itself.*"

Loki was probing now.

Or perhaps *shaking things up* was a better phrase.

The real reason Loki had aggressively pushed to be the host this month was for this opportunity—a chance to look straight into the eyes of all those assembled and gauge their reactions. She was hoping for some kind of clue as to just who was behind the events surrounding the recent Monsterphilia, the eighteenth floor, and the twenty-fourth-floor pantry.

Something to connect the flesh-eating viola flowers, the crystal orb fetus, the half-human, half-monster creatures, and the remnants of the Evils.

The intensely hued monsters Aiz and the others had first faced on their previous expedition could have easily overthrown the whole city if they pleased. This grave reason was what spurred Loki into gradually involving herself more and more with Dionysus and Hermes's little scheme since their secret meeting in the bar a few days prior, and the same reason they were laying their trap now.

The plan was to smoke out the suspects.

In my opinion, every single god in this city is a suspect—and an enemy of my children.

Dionysus had remarked, still feeling the sting of his own lost followers.

Villains were unfortunately plentiful in the ranks of the gods, and Loki found herself unable to deny his assertion. Every single god and goddess at the round table was a suspect.

One of them could be the mastermind behind everything—the destroyer of cities, "Enyo."

There was a corrupt god among them. One with allies underground in the Dungeon as well as on the surface, aligned with the surviving Evils.

Loki and the others would be using this month's Denatus to investigate the identity of this leader as well as his or her accomplices.

It would be tonight, at this banquet for the city's most powerful gods.

"Watch yourselves, everyone, 'cause I've also heard tell about some naughty little good-for-nothin' reprobates scuttlin' around and makin' a nuisance of themselves lately."

Loki's scarlet eyes narrowed as a thin smile graced her lips, her nose sniffing for that undeniable stench that could come from only an Evil.

Dionysus and Hermes, too, kept their eyes alert for any suspicious behavior among those seated at the table.

The newcomers to the mortal plane—those who'd been in Orario for only two or three years now—suspiciously examined those around the table while the rest of the women exaggeratedly brought their hands to their mouths and mumbled, "Well, you know…" and the men snickered among themselves with sardonic expressions, saying, "Sooo scaaary."

The probing had begun in earnest, and now every deity was involved.

"Can I say something, too?!"

A voice.

From a table rose a finely sculpted bronze arm.

It was followed by the owner himself—none other than Ganesha, the god in the elephant mask.

"First, let me just start by saying…I am Ganesha!"

"Yeah, yeah, we got it. Sit down already."

"No, no, that's not what I meant to say! I wanted to start by apologizing for the debacle at the Monsterphilia!" Ganesha corrected himself after Loki's insulting brush-off. "But you must understand— I swear on the name of Ganesha, Lord of Hosts, that those violas you speak of are not related to my familia! You must believe me!!" He continued from atop his chair, constantly changing his pose.

Ganesha Familia had cooperated with the Guild to host Monsterphilia. The elephant-masked god was using this opportunity here at Denatus to apologize ardently for letting those monsters run wild during the event, as well as recognizing the efforts of another god and her followers who worked to bring the commotion under control.

Loki subtly shifted her attention to one person who had been responsible for at least half of the mess in the first place—the silver-haired goddess of beauty, who was currently sipping a cup of tea she had received from a divine fan of hers.

Ganesha wanted to make it very clear that he knew nothing about the monsters involved in the incident.

"And another thing! Those same monsters down on the eighteenth floor killed some of my followers, too! I have no idea whether the two incidents are related, but I would very much like to avenge my children!! If anyone has any information, I ask wholeheartedly that you bring it forward!" Ganesha slammed his fist on the table.

He referred now to the top-secret quest one of his followers, Hashana Dorlia, had been given to retrieve the crystal-orb fetus, and which ultimately had gotten him killed by the crimson-haired creature Levis.

A pair of tears rolled out from the bottom of the aggrieved deity's elephant mask, tracing the curves of his cheeks.

Seeing the normally eccentric god actually shedding tears was enough to make the other gods stop short, their mouths clamping shut.

"Why...*why*, Hashana?! To be killed during coitus...! To be seduced by a bombshell only to lose his life—*ah!* I'm so jealous! Why couldn't that have been me?!"

"The hell? Hashana didn't kick the bucket while he was getting it on," Loki interjected as Ganesha continued to weep hot tears of envy.

"What?"

Somehow or another, the god had gotten the impression that his follower had been slain while in the arms of a buxom beauty.

Loki stared indifferently at the ridiculous elephant mask adorning the god's face. The temporary suspense that had seized the room was broken in an instant by Ganesha's characteristic banality.

Sigh. "Typical...!" Loki exclaimed as a strange atmosphere settled over the room.

Throwing a quick glance at Dionysus and Hermes, both of whom were smiling wryly, she decided to halt the search here and return to the real matter at hand.

"Anyone have anything else to say? We all good?" she asked, assuming her hostly duties again.

From the indifference of her peers, it seemed everyone was fresh out of gossip. She scanned the circumference of the table...then decided to carry on as planned.

Lips curling upward, she returned to her usual antics.

"Well then, let's carry on, shall we? Time for the naming ceremony."

Almost instantaneously, a strange sense of tension gripped the room.

The moment the words had passed from her lips, the faces of the gods and goddesses who'd yet to participate in the conversation grew pale, the young, busty goddess next to Hephaistos included.

Loki smirked together with the other Denatus regulars, the lot of them boasting their most depraved smiles of the day.

The real feast, the farce, was about to begin.

"All reports have been shared proper, yeah? Then let's get started! Lessee now, our top batter for today is…Seti of *Ceto Familia!*"

"P-please go easy on me…!!"

"""""""""""*Denied!*"""""""""""

"Noooooooooooooo*oooooooooooooooo*————!!"

It was time to bequeath aliases upon the newly leveled-up adventurers—the monthly naming ceremony.

Every adventurer's official nickname was decided at Denatus, from Aiz's "Sword Princess" to Tiona's "Amazon."

These aliases, as they were called, were names bequeathed by the gods, meant to extol the exploits of the mortal recipient. They signified the official recognition of deusdea, acting as a symbol of the strength and renown of the chosen adventurer.

Those on the lower world who'd not yet been able to attain one of these refined names from the gods viewed their compatriots with respect and envy.

"All right! Adventurer Erika Rosalia…nickname, Violante!"

"Nooooooooooooooooooooooooooooooooooooo!!"

However, the gods themselves did not view this venerable custom with the same excitement as their arguably old-fashioned children. In fact, they wanted to avoid it like the plague.

The majority of aliases born from the naming ceremony were names of complete and utter tragedy meant to make the adventurer's patron deity writhe in discomfort. For a god to see the child they had so carefully raised receive a stigma-inducing name that would become the butt of every joke—it was enough for some to pass out in agony. There was no greater torture in existence.

For the especially mean-spirited gods, seeing an adventurer all proud and haughty about their freshly minted title while their patron deity squirmed in torment was one of the greatest pleasures in all the world and exactly why they couldn't stop.

As Loki filtered suggestions, took votes, and finally handed down each new name—or perhaps *death sentence* would be a better phrase—to its unsuspecting adventurer, the patron deities in question howled and wailed in utter despair.

Now that the ceremony's begun, maybe we can end this on a happy note?

Loki thought to herself as each of the low-level gods at the meeting was subjected to the usual hazing. Though what she really wanted to do was probe a bit further and see whether she could gauge any more reactions, she knew that would be asking for too much.

These thoughts running through her head, she dutifully carried on as host.

"Have we decided on a name for Mikoto Yamato yet? If not, let's hurry it up!"

"Not yet! I haven't gotten rid of my karma and suffering from the last ceremony—Angelic Code, the Eternal Virgin Revelations!!"

"Jeanne of Yamato, the Divine Wind of the Far East!"

"Saint Tail, the Holy Spy!"

"You fools! The only real choice here is Salty Angel, the Lovingly Raised!"

"Stop it, stop it, *stop iiiiiiiiiiiiiiitttttttttttttttttttttttttttttttttttt*!!"

The round-table debate was really hitting a climax now as the patron deity of the poor hostage adventurer kept wailing in horror. Loki turned her gaze away as the twin-bunned god brought his hands to both sides of his head with great gulping sobs.

Catching her gaze, Dionysus simply shrugged. His subsequent sigh seemed to state the obvious—that their efforts had achieved nothing.

"Dionysus, you're looking pretty smug over there. Care to join the conversation?"

"Yeah! You actually decided to attend for once, so why not toss out a suggestion, hm?"

"We've got quite the task in front of us. Coming up with an alias for that rookie Mikoto who everyone's been talking about!"

"Oh? Let me think..." Dionysus replied upon instigation from his peers.

All eyes on him, he took a glance at the report on the table and the profile the Guild had created for the adventurer in preparation for her naming. The parchment revealed a beautiful girl from the Far East with jet-black hair.

Dionysus smiled ever so sweetly.

"How about Eternal Shadow?"

"Dionysus, you bastaaaaaaaaaaaaaaaaaaaaaaaaaaaaaaaaaaaaaaaaaaaard!!"

Once again, this month's Denatus wouldn't disappoint.

"All right, then! Mikoto's title is now...Eternal Shadow!"

"No objections here!" "None from me!" "Sounds good!"

"No, no, no, *nooooooooooooooooooooooooooooooooooooo*!!"

The warrior god let out a defeated cry as the votes were cast, solidifying Dionysus's proposal.

Soon out-of-control laughter from his fellow gods followed. As the grand circus claimed its newest victim, Loki thought to herself of the fun she'd be having soon, as well.

Once the small to medium familias had done their time in the lower reaches of hell, the names of newly leveled-up adventurers from elite familias would be next. The abhorrent aliases would decrease remarkably, no doubt to keep fights from breaking out among the most influential gods and goddesses of the city as their second-tier-plus adventurers were considered. *Hephaistos Familia*, *Ganesha Familia*, and *Ishtar Familia* all had names on the list.

She was able to get through them with naught but a single argument from a certain goddess.

"Let's steer things back on track, yeah? Next is..." she said with a snicker, "...a big name! My very own Aiz!"

"The Sword Princess arrives at last!!"

"And still as beautiful as ever, to boot."

"Level Six already? Impressive..."

Loki's own follower was up, and all eyes were on her.

It was her golden-haired, golden-eyed swordswoman, boasting the same level of fame and renown as the three leaders of *Loki Familia* and even matching the current apex of Orario, an adventurer known as the Warlord.

Considering the insane progress she had made in a little over ten short years, simply mentioning the girl had been enough to reinvigorate the room.

The Sword Princess, Aiz Wallenstein, had finally joined the ranks of the Level 6s.

"The little lady has really outdone herself this time." One of the gods smiled, seemingly overcome with joy, at the sight of the doll-like girl and her achievements on the parchment in front of them. The last part of the report was reserved for background details regarding her level-up, which, in Aiz's case, was her victory over Udaeus, the Monster Rex of the thirty-seventh floor.

To defeat a floor boss single-handedly was a mighty feat, and the revelation put the whole room in a state of feverish elation.

"She beat that thing all on her own? Gods almighty, that girl is dangerous! Even more than Ottar!"

"I wouldn't say that. Ottar had his own expedition and almost brought down the floor boss Parole by himself. I'd still say he's more of a force to be reckoned with."

"But for Udaeus to be laid low..."

"Heh, well, he's the weakest of the four generals anyway..."

"Quite a disgrace to lose to our idol like that..."

"Hey! Quit picking on Mister Udaeus!!"

"Yeah, he's the strongest of the four generals! So quit with the bad-mouthing!"

Words of praise and admiration flew back and forth around the table.

Even the young, buxom goddess sitting alongside Hephaistos found herself groaning in spite of herself at the sheer magnitude of the young adventurer's feat.

"We've got more-important things to worry about than Udaeus now. C'mon, we've gotta think of a new alias!"

"Hmm..."

"But do we really need to change hers? Seems a bit silly if there's no reason to."

"Indeed."

"If we were to change it...perhaps something like Sword Saint?"

"Sword...Saint?"

"Doesn't really seem to fit her, though, you think?"

"I don't know about you guys, but clearly the only viable candidate I see is Our Wife."

"*It's perfect!*" the voices chorused from around the room.

The general ruckus showed no signs of waning, and the gods proceeded at once with the naming, fully prepared to change Aiz's alias from Sword Princess to Our Wife.

Until.

"I will murder every last one of you."

The suggestion was effectively rejected by a single glare from Loki.

"*W-we're so sorry!!*" the voices chorused once again.

The goddess's ice-cold scowl was enough to inform them that they'd crossed a line, and every single god in the room quickly brought their forehead to the table in fervent apology.

Loki would surely bring about the destruction of anyone and everyone who'd dare give one of her adorable children a disgraceful name. Her love for them was just that strong.

The gods had incurred the wrath of the most influential god in all of Orario, and their fear of being sent back to heaven was enough to force them to their knees in concession.

"Really now. You should learn to pick yer fights better. Anyway, let's carry on..." She cleared her throat, turning over Aiz's report with a little flick and glancing down at the final piece of parchment. "We have only one left, it seems."

The profile now reflected in her eyes belonged to a decidedly nervous-looking human boy.

So that shorty's brat actually managed to level up, huh?

Her brows furrowed as she saw the words *Hestia Familia* beneath his image.

Honestly, it wasn't too big a surprise, considering the small goddess herself was participating in the month's Denatus, but it didn't mean Loki had to like it.

No, definitely not.

And to make matters worse…it only took him a month and a half? What in the world???

She wondered as she glanced at the "days required" section from among the short summary of information.

The sight of that brazenly printed number had her groaning inwardly, just like Hestia herself had a couple of minutes prior. And yet, for some reason, she found her antipathy laced with suspicion.

Aiz's record aside, this is impossible! There's no way he could've done this in only a month and a half.

She thought back to eight years ago.

When a certain eight-year-old girl who hadn't known her place rose to Level 2 at an absolutely outrageous pace.

She needed only a year. That was how fast Aiz had done it, and even that had been an incredible feat, setting a record that had yet to be broken by anyone else in the whole world.

Until today.

Even if this isn't some type of treachery, to think that Itty-Bitty's kid just…just…ohhhh, aaaarrrghhhhh!!

She must have falsified the record.

Either that or he'd already collected excelia before registering as a lower-class adventurer with the Guild and been falsely reported as a rookie.

There were really many ways of circumventing the system if someone was so inclined.

That being said, the young goddess, Hestia, didn't seem like the type who'd do something that stupid—a fact that Loki had to accept despite the cat-and-dog relationship the two shared.

Which meant that this boy had truly accomplished an unprecedented feat.

A feat that, according to the short history recorded on the parchment, involved taking down a minotaur.

"…The rabbit set a new record."

Loki's ears perked up at the murmur of a certain gentlemanly god, his eyes narrowed as he surveyed the parchment from the other side of the table.

Yes, the other gods would need to give this final adventurer—this little rabbit, as it were—an alias, a thought that had Loki practically licking her lips in anticipation, though she was ultimately able to maintain her stoic expression.

Still, this kid's growth…this is definitely gonna require some investigatin'.

The whispers of her peers flew back and forth across the table.

Shooting a glance at Hestia, seemingly preparing herself to fight for a "safe" name for her follower, Loki quietly rose to her feet.

"…Loki?"

"Before we decide on an alias, I wanna ask Itty-Bitty a question," she stated, looking straight at Hestia and ignoring the reactions of the gods around her. Her crimson eyes widened. "What were you thinking, lettin' this kid level up after only a month and a half?"

Bam.

Her fist came down on the table directly atop the boy's report, her voice as intimidating as possible. She didn't miss the way the throat of the other goddess bobbed with a tiny gulp in response.

"Not even my Aiz could do it that fast. It took her a year. A year! So tell me, huh? How'd this boy do it in only a month and a half? What kinda hoax you tryin' to pull here?"

"…"

"Our Blessin's ain't supposed to be used for that. Whaddaya think'd happen if we had all our kids level up after only a month or so, huh? The fact that they can't certainly puts 'em through a lot of trouble."

"……"

"Well, c'mon! Say something, Itty-Bitty!"

"………"

Ever-increasing drips of sweat began sliding down Hestia's face, but whether or not her insides were all aflutter, as well, her exterior remained as stiff as a statue.

There was no way Loki could believe it.

The speed at which the boy had advanced was absolutely ridiculous, and there had to be something decidedly abnormal at play.

Something akin to the beastly creature Levis, for instance—an enhanced species.

Perhaps the secret behind the boy's growth was thanks to "her," the being that Olivas Act had spoken of and the very same authority Loki and the others were facing.

Loki's eyes searched every inch of that buxom young goddess for an answer.

Just in case, you know?

She reasoned it out to herself, though she knew she had nothing to back up her suspicions.

The very idea that the Evils would be connected to a follower of Hestia, the most birdbrained, blockheaded goddess Loki knew, was enough to turn the entire world upside down. It was such a preposterous assumption that a serious investigation might very well make Loki shrivel up and die.

Which was why this look into enhanced species and all that was only an addendum. She mostly just wanted to screw with Hestia.

She was certainly mad that one of the tiny goddess's children could have broken her Aiz's record. Also, to be honest, she was a little bit curious how he had managed it.

If she had to take a guess, a skill, maybe. A rare, undocumented skill that could increase the rate of growth.

This instigated a wide variety of emotions in her as a god, and they swirled around her mind as she continued her cross-examination of Hestia.

"You gonna talk or what? It couldn't be...that you used our powers to do it, could it?"

"O-of course I didn't! I would never!"

By "used our powers," Loki was, of course, referring to the use of

Arcanum, the power of the gods, to "mod" her follower's structure—an accusation that was more to stir the pot than one that had any real substance.

Loki knew all too well.

The moment that gods began breaking rules and used their Arcanum to mod their followers was the moment everything would become completely and utterly boring. Nothing would have meaning anymore. It was an act that would defile the very game they'd created in this world, and the entire thing would lose its splendor for her and everyone else.

If someone truly wanted to throw away their life with their adorable children and live in the lap of luxury again, all any god needed to do was return to heaven, where nothing but debauchery-filled days awaited.

No, that wasn't what the gods had had in mind when they started this game.

Nearly every god had high hopes that one of the children they'd bestowed their Blessings upon would eventually become a hero.

"All right then, tell us! Should be easy if you've got nothin' to hide, yeah?"

"Gngh..."

Loki's words left Hestia no room to escape.

The gaze of every god and goddess at Denatus focused on her.

Quiet had seized the room as everyone's interest was piqued, and the young goddess didn't have a single person covering for her, not even Hephaistos, who sat directly next to her with a frown on her face.

Loki didn't care how she felt, though—she was going to get an explanation for the boy's uncanny growth whether Hestia wanted to give it or not.

"Really now. Is it that important?"

At least, she would have.

Until a lilting, soprano voice cut through the air between the two of them.

"...Huh?"

"What'd you say?"

© Kiyotaka Haimura

First Hestia, then Loki, then everyone in the room turned their eyes toward the source of the voice. Toward the alluring yet disinterested features of the silver-haired goddess of beauty.

"So long as Hestia's not doing anything wrong, I see no reason to choke the answer out of her like this. The business of a familia is just that—its own business. And discussing our followers' statuses has always been taboo, has it not?" Freya continued, entirely disenchanted, and Loki's eyes narrowed in suspicion at the infuriating goddess she couldn't seem to rid herself of.

"...One month. Do you even understand what that means, you perverted goddess?"

Freya just chuckled. "Why so stubborn, Loki? If anything, you're the one acting strange here."

You're the one breaking taboo were the words left unsaid, and the smug goddess followed up with a pretentious smile as though she'd just noticed this implication herself.

"You're not jealous, are you, dear? All because Hestia's follower broke the record of your precious little darling?"

"Like hell I am!" Loki responded instantly to the completely truthful accusation, although she nearly gulped.

"Is that so?" Freya merely smiled, goading her on.

Loki's eyes went red. Ready to verbally lash the other goddess, she suddenly found herself unable to move, trapped by the gaze of those silver eyes.

This unbearable woman, is she...?

If she wanted to play the blame game and twist her words like this, Loki was fully prepared to go head-to-head. However, she could tell already that anything she said now would only get her wrapped tighter and tighter within Freya's coils.

She stuck her tongue out in spite of herself, and Freya responded with a coy smile.

"It's true that I can scarcely believe it myself, just looking at the number. It must be some kind of miracle!"

"But he did take down that minotaur. That's a miracle in and of itself, isn't it? He completely overcame their difference in levels."

"If we must apply logic to it, perhaps the creature was some kind of fated rival of the boy's, so the excelia he received upon defeating it held a special significance?"

"Leveling up after something like that isn't beyond the realm of possibility...or at least that's what I think."

The other gods and goddesses began tossing around ideas of their own, inspired by Freya's comment.

Just like Loki, Freya was a goddess of one of the largest familias in Orario and, as such, an influential voice. Adding in her sheer charm—which had earned her a reputation as an incarnation of beauty itself—she was quickly amassing support even now.

"I stand behind Lady Freya!" Hermes piped up, cementing his own reputation as a spineless coward, and Dionysus was forced to let out a sigh.

Wait. This doesn't have anythin' to do with what she said that night, does it? Maybe the kid Freya's after is actually...? Loki pondered, memories of a certain evening inhabiting the back of her mind as Freya's suggestion was met with more and more approval.

It had been the night of the Monsterphilia, when Loki met with Freya for their secret meeting in a high-class pub within the city's Shopping District.

"If you're willing to stay quiet about today's events...I'll offer you the robe for your silence. Do we have a deal?"

They'd made an agreement that day.

Loki had threatened to go to the Guild with a report about the goddess of beauty's antics at Monsterphilia but had ultimately been done in by her own weakness and begrudgingly agreed to keep things under wraps.

Specifically, Loki had promised to hold back everything relating to the kid Freya had fallen for.

She'd turned a blind eye then, she would have to again in the future, and she had to now as well.

With that one look from Freya's otherworldly gaze, Loki understood. Freya was infatuated with none other than the very child they were discussing—Hestia's follower.

Then the kid's fight with the minotaur that Ishtar mentioned…that was Freya's doing, too?

While she couldn't be sure whether Freya'd already been able to see the kid's potential for growth at the time, she'd certainly zeroed in on him pretty quickly, which would explain why she was covering for him now in front of the rest of the gods, as if he was her personal plaything.

Loki could taste bile in her mouth.

Don't interfere, those silver eyes had practically whispered, and Loki knew she had no choice—she was going to have to let all of Freya's actions regarding the boy, Bell Cranell, go unchecked, no matter how much it pained her to do so.

Thus, the explanation for Bell Cranell's uncanny growth would remain a mystery, just as Freya wished.

That kid's gotta be somethin' if even Freya's taken an interest. I mean, with a stupid record like this…but didn't she call him a transparent, unreliable crybaby?…Ugh, whatever! I still don't like it!

Loki felt flames lick at her insides as she grumbled to herself, completely unaware of the discussion currently taking place among the men regarding the boy's new alias—a discussion the women in the room withdrew from with apathetic disinterest.

No. Agreement or not, she did not like being someone's toy. With a start, she flew from her chair, disregarding what was happening around the table and dashing over to Hestia, who had a very dim-witted look on her face.

"…Loki?" Hestia glanced up upon Loki's arrival.

"…Watch yerself, Itty-Bitty," Loki murmured sullenly.

"Huh?"

"I'm tellin' you to keep yer eyes open. I can't even believe I'm tellin' ya this, but…I can't stand seein' that tramp play around with people like this," she continued. "She's making a fool outta ya."

Apparently irritated, Loki raised her head and looked away from Hestia.

She was focused on the goddess just now leaving her seat.

Those long silver locks of hers passed through the doorway to the hall and disappeared from view.

"W-wait just a second! What is that supposed to mean, 'watch yourself'? What am I watching?!"

"Don'tcha get it, you moron? That chick's taken your boy under her wing!"

"Y-you mean Freya?" Hestia asked, raising her voice. Her blue eyes darted to and fro with confusion.

Loki, however, merely righted herself with a snort.

"You...you really don't get it? Ignorance is bliss, I guess. Well... whatever. Not like it's got anythin' to do with me!" she finished apathetically before returning to her seat.

While the thought of giving any sort of advice to that buxom rival of hers was enough to make her blood boil, she hated seeing her fall prey to Freya's whims even more, so she was willing to try just about anything.

Even giving a (begrudging) warning to her sworn enemy.

After returning to her seat, Loki didn't have more than a brief moment to settle in before—

""""""""""""""*We've got it!!*"""""""""""""""

—the final adventurer's alias was chosen, and the naming ceremony came to a close.

The Denatus ended without any further hitches.

The deities in attendance made their way out of the great hall one by one, a number of them on their way to Guild Headquarters in high spirits to officially announce the results of the naming ceremony.

Once all had left and the hall was deserted, only Loki, Dionysus, and Hermes remained.

"So...either of you see anyone suspicious?"

"While there were, indeed, a few who caught my eye...I'm more inclined to believe they were simply reveling in others' misfortunes rather than exposing themselves as the ones responsible. Some people just want to watch the world burn."

"Pretty much the same here."

Dionysus and Hermes reported their unfavorable news respectively, the former dressed in a fine nobleman's suit and the latter donning a set of lightweight traveling clothes.

Loki exchanged glances with the members of her unlikely trio from her seat atop the round table.

Nothin', huh? Well...guess we weren't expectin' much anyway.

It was hard to believe the mastermind instigating recent events would even dare attend a Denatus in the first place. And even someone with the audacity to make an appearance wouldn't be foolish enough to show their true colors.

It woulda been a real find if there was a person who actually knew anything, Loki thought to herself, feeling no real sense of failure or discouragement and simply grumbling for the sake of grumbling.

"And after all the trouble I went to, too..."

Not that I didn't have all the time in the world, what with Aiz and the others gone, she added silently.

"I'll make sure to have some fine wines sent to your place, yes?" Dionysus answered with a wry smile at Loki's look of malcontent, hoping it might appease the goddess.

"Well, I'll be off, then."

Hermes cut in suddenly.

"Whaaaaat?" Loki spun around.

"I've got some minor business to attend to, and I must leave the city posthaste. Preparations have already been made for the trip," Hermes replied casually, wearing his omnipresent gentlemanly smile. He glanced down at the piece of parchment in his hand and the list of leveled-up adventurers. "I've procured myself quite the story for the journey, too," he murmured to himself, crinkling his already narrow eyes. "At any rate, I leave Orario in your capable hands while I'm out. What? Don't give me that look! I'll be back before you know it, and we'll be able to continue this little matter of ours then. I've already instructed my followers to begin collecting information. I'll see you both later. Ta-ta!"

The impish god supplied no more details than necessary before donning his feathered traveling cap, waving good-bye with a smile, and departing.

"Wasn't he the one calling himself just as much a victim as us...?" Loki's brows furrowed as Dionysus narrowed his gaze.

"Well, that's Hermes for you."

"Speaking of, aren't the two of you from the same region up in heaven?"

"As much as I wish that we were not," Dionysus responded with a tired sigh. "Though, correct me if I'm wrong, that is true of you and that Hestia you were so suspicious of, as well, hm?"

The two of them threw identical looks of annoyance in the direction in which their tryingly capricious accomplices had disappeared.

"Has it really been ten days since then...?" Loki murmured from atop her cushiony sofa in the parlor room of *Loki Familia*'s home, Twilight Manor.

The dwarven marionettes on the automaton clock began to move, signaling the morning hour. The clock itself, along with a nearby music box, was one of many antiques decorating the orange room.

Memories of the Denatus from several days prior and what was going on behind that sham of a banquet ran through Loki's head as she stared upward at the ceiling...before it all quickly fizzled out entirely.

"There's nothin' to dooooooo...I don't even wanna get up..." Hands behind her head, she let her legs flop lazily over the edge of the sofa. She reached toward the nearby round table and the glass there, bringing the wine—which had been delivered, as promised, by one of Dionysus's followers after Denatus—to her lips and gulping it down all at once.

She drew a number of looks from familia members passing by the room, those who hadn't left for the expedition. They viewed their patron deity's morning alcoholism with equal parts shock and amazement.

"Wonder if Aiz and the others'll be back soon..." she mumbled absently into the room, which suddenly felt cavernous and lacking in female companionship. It was clear from Loki's voice that she harbored no doubts as to her followers' safe return.

"—Loki! Bete has returned!"

"Oh?"

Speak of the devil.

Hearing the sudden call from one of her followers out in the hallway facing the parlor room, Loki popped up into a sitting position on her sofa. She hurried after the messenger toward the manor's main entrance.

Wait, by "Bete," you don't mean...only Bete, do you? she thought to herself with a little cock of her head as she entered the vast entrance hall, only to see the werewolf standing there alone.

The tattered state of his battle gear was a dead giveaway that he'd just returned from the Dungeon.

"Hey hey, Bete! Welcome back!" Loki exclaimed, fully prepared to launch herself on the werewolf despite the circumstances.

"Ah, can it! I still got things to do!" Bete answered with a well-placed sidestep, avoiding the goddess's embrace. Instead, as though severely pressed for time, he grabbed the nearest junior members who had come to greet him, instructing them to "Bring everyone here right now! And make it fast!"

"R-roger!" they answered in stammered confusion before running off to obey his menacing command. Loki watched this play out before asking the question she'd wanted to ask since she learned of his arrival.

"Hey. Where are Finn and the others?"

Between additional orders for a backpack and meat as he made ready to head back out, Bete replied. After recounting how the entire expedition was holed up on the eighteenth floor, paralyzed by the many injured who had fallen victim to poison-vermis attacks, he explained that he needed to gather up as much of the antidote as he could find and bring it all back down into the Dungeon.

"I see." Loki responded to the werewolf's succinct summary of events with a nod.

"I'm headed to *Dian Cecht Familia*. Even if I buy up every dose they have, it probably won't be enough, so have Rox and the others start goin' around to item shops."

"Okay! Should take, what...two, three days?"

Poison vermis inhabited only the lower levels, and even then they were usually not very numerous, meaning antivenin made from their secretions would be hard to come by. Even if they scoured the entire city, there was no guarantee they'd be able to find what they needed. If the stores didn't have enough in stock and their human-wave tactics to find more failed, the only option left would be to commission *Dian Cecht Familia* to craft them some more.

There was, of course, always the option of asking Dea Saint, renowned for her advanced healing magic, to personally venture into the Dungeon and help the afflicted...but that would cost even more than the prohibitively expensive antivenin. While Amid would no doubt be happy to discreetly lend her aid in order to help Aiz and the others, the real problem was her patron deity, Dian Cecht. He was liable to take full advantage of the situation just as he'd done during one of their previous quests—he already charged an arm and a leg for the medical procedures Amid normally performed at their clinic.

Loki understood all of this as she listened to Bete barking out orders, and she traced an invisible check mark in the air with her finger.

"Sure ya don't need to rest a bit, Bete? You must be bone-tired, fresh out of the Dungeon like that. Need me ta massage those broad shoulders of yers?" Loki waggled her fingers as she made a beeline for Bete's backside.

Bete, however, only shot her a dirty look. "Enough already! I'm fine." Shrugging on the backpack one of the familia members had brought him and gnawing voraciously at a hunk of meat still on the bone, he suddenly began rummaging through his battle jacket, almost as though a thought had just occurred to him.

He pulled out a rolled-up piece of parchment. "Oh yeah. Loki," he said, turning around.

"Whazzat?"

"It's from Finn. Read it yer damn self," he called as he headed for the door.

Loki glanced down at the neatly scrawled red print, a smile forming on her lips.

Finn's handwriting detailed what had taken place on the fifty-ninth floor—"her" true form, the corrupted spirit, as well as the plot their enemies were currently concocting to bring down Orario.

"You did good, Bete," Loki said with a smile as she watched the werewolf's receding form leave the manor behind.

CHAPTER 2

Rabbit Rookie

Гэта казка іншага сям'і.

◆

Трусік Навічок

Back on the eighteenth floor, the Under Resort.

The bluish veil of artificial night had been lifted as the glimmer of morning crystal settled down atop the safety point. Its soft glow blanketed everything, from the wetlands in the north to the forest spreading far to the east and south, covering the relay town atop the island in the lake to the west as well.

Within that swath of underground land lay *Loki Familia*'s base camp, erected along the southern tip of the forest.

As the inhabitants of the camp began to rise, so did the noise level as they went about their morning duties.

"Wh-what's happened, Mister Raul?"

"Huh? Oh, Lefiya."

Lefiya frantically made her way toward Raul in the crowd of people at the center of camp. Her long auburn hair was loose instead of in its typical ponytail, evidence that she'd only just gotten up.

The young elf had been fast asleep inside her tent until the commotion outside woke her and she rushed out to see what was the matter. Incidentally, the two Amazonian sisters, with their animalistic sensitivity to all things to do with blood and battle, were still fast asleep back in the tent, completely unaware of the alarm gripping their camp.

Raul, along with Aki next to him, turned around to face the approaching elf.

"Some adventurers came down from the seventeenth floor. Miss Aiz found them passed out by the stairs and saved them..." Raul replied.

"Seems like ol' Goliath had his way with them...they're banged up pretty good and still out cold," Aki added.

The group had formed a circle around the three adventurers in question, who were asleep on the grass as Riveria, Leene, and the other healers cared for them, constantly monitoring their conditions.

They were dressed casually in robes with inner linens fashioned from salamander wool, all of them decidedly worse for wear. Aiz herself sat among the healers, her usual stoic expression overcome with worry as she watched them work.

"Seems like one of 'em is from *Hephaistos Familia*," Aki mused as she took in the scene before focusing on a corner of the crowd where a cotton-swathe-clad Tsubaki stood together with her small group of poison-afflicted smiths.

"Oh, Welfy…" the half-dwarf high smith murmured, her right eye (the one not covered by its usual eye patch) staring at the scarlet-haired boy.

While it was an unwritten rule of the Dungeon that parties were supposed to leave one another well enough alone, given that one of the injured was a member of their allied familia, there was clearly no way *Loki Familia* could ignore their plight.

And it was a plight. Even as low as they were on resources upon their return from their expedition, *Loki Familia* wasn't so heartless and narrow-minded as to abandon their fellow adventurers in a time of great need.

At Riveria's prompt instruction, the red-haired boy's bandages and armaments were removed and his broken leg splinted, the warm glimmer of healing spells surrounding him.

"Ah, right. And then there's Miss Aiz's friend," Raul added almost as an afterthought.

"Miss Aiz's…?"

Lefiya's senses tingled at those words.

Finally, she took a good, long look at the injured adventurers lying on the grass.

She first saw a young prum girl, followed by the human smith Tsubaki was so worried about, and lastly, though his face was hidden by the shadow of Aiz's frame, she saw a human boy…

…*Hm?*

The sight gave her an uncanny sense of foreboding.

In the next instant, she found herself winding through the crowd, azure eyes straining with all their might—staring at the boy on the ground. Aiz's hand was resting softly on his forehead.

Those slender limbs, that slight frame, his features and their immutably cherubic innocence...and finally, that pure-white hair, as white as snow.

Lefiya's eyes widened with an almost audible *snap*.

"Hngggggaaaaaaaaaaaaaaaaaahhhhhhhhh?!"

She stood frozen with her finger pointed straight at the boy.

The horrendous scream squeezed from her throat was enough to make not only Raul, Aki, and the other familia members stop in their tracks but Riveria and Aiz, as well.

It was none other than her (self-declared) fated rival, the boy she'd shared her beloved mentor with in the days leading up to the expedition.

Once again, luck had brought her face-to-face with her arch-enemy, Bell Cranell.

"Lefiya, you will be quiet!"

"I-I apologize!"

Riveria's wrath immediately fell upon her.

Soft sleeping breaths permeated the tent.

The firmly closed eyelids of slumbering patients told of the predicament they'd so narrowly escaped. Half-hidden beneath their blankets, the boy, young man, and girl lay fast asleep atop simple beds fashioned for them from outer garments.

Aiz was sitting on the floor, examining the faces of Bell and the other members of his party under the pretense of nursing them.

Half a day's time had passed since Aiz had carried them back to *Loki Familia*'s base camp. They were in Finn's tent, the captain surrendering his space willingly after he learned the situation. After checking in on them earlier, he had instructed her to bring the adventurers to the main tent once they'd awoken, if at all possible. Tsubaki and the other *Hephaistos Familia* smiths also dropped by occasionally to check on the young man who seemed to be their companion.

Thanks to the efforts of Riveria and the other healers, their wounds had been fully mended. Even the young man's broken leg, the worst of the injuries, had been restored. The power of strong healing magic and meticulous care was truly impressive. The remaining light scratches and bruises had been treated with what little ointments and bandages remained.

Aiz lowered her eyes toward the white strips of cloth veiling the face of the boy sleeping by her folded knees.

You already made it all this way...?

Voices and laughter drifted in through the tent's sheets every now and then as her fingers combed through the boy's bangs.

With most of their items and armor no longer covering their bodies, the unconscious adventurers were an especially sorry sight. They must have been running for their lives, forcing themselves through the middle levels and finally arriving at the eighteenth floor by the skin of their teeth.

It had been only two weeks since she'd last parted with him.

At the time, he had been a Level-1 lower-class adventurer, and she was certain at one point during their training together on the city walls he'd told her the deepest he'd ever gone was the tenth floor.

And yet, here they were, a scant fourteen days later, and he'd already raised that count by eight.

From the upper levels to the middle levels in the blink of an eye.

It was unbelievable. A speed that was enough to make her doubt her own ears.

But the fact that they were here now, lying right in front of her, was proof enough, and she was forced to acknowledge her astonishment.

He's Level 2 now...

The adventure he'd completed, that cutthroat battle with the minotaur, had caused him to level up, and he'd broken free of his previous level.

Just as Aiz had done with her subjugation of Udaeus.

At least he must have, otherwise it would have been virtually impossible for him to make it all the way to the eighteenth floor.

No doubt, he and his party members hadn't originally planned on descending to this safety point. She could only guess that they'd run into something unexpected while exploring the shallow reaches of the middle levels, preventing their return to the surface—an incident that made it impossible for them to escape the Dungeon's halls.

A massive cave-in along one of the main routes? Or a pitfall, perhaps, that they accidentally dropped into after some monster hounded them. These types of things weren't uncommon in the Cave Labyrinth, the area also known as the "first line," often considered a threshold to a great increase in danger.

And so the three adventurers, faced with one of these deplorable situations…hadn't relied on luck. They had not waited for help that may or may not have come. No, they'd pressed on so they could return home with their lives.

"You wanted to save them, didn't you…?"

She remembered his tragically heroic face as he'd pleaded for her to save his companions, right before he'd passed out completely.

It had been courage, determination, wisdom, and selflessness in the face of certain death that had led Bell and the others to this safety point.

"…But…"

—You shouldn't push yourself so.

Ignoring the fact that this was advice she, herself, needed to heed, she reached a hand toward Bell's face.

There'd been so much blood pouring from his forehead and staining his body. Even now, the scars were still visible, and his face remained tormented with fatigue.

She lowered her golden eyes, gently caressing the strips of gauze on his forehead.

When suddenly—

"…Ngh."

"!"

—his eyelids fluttered, almost as though he was receiving life from Aiz's touch.

Aiz withdrew her hand in an instant.

It seemed as if he was struggling against an overwhelming feeling of weakness when the slightest of moans passed between his lips.

She stared at his face until finally, the rabbit's brilliant rubellite eyes cracked open.

" ... "

Ever so slowly, his eyelids rose. He blinked once. Twice.

He seemed not to notice Aiz sitting beside him at all. Instead, he simply stared at the ceiling of the tent as though unsure he'd awoken.

But then—

"—Lilly. Welf?!"

His eyes popped wide open as he sat straight up in bed.

He jerked forward, having seemingly no recollection of what had transpired, fully prepared to jump to his feet and come to his companions' aid, when—

Ah! You shouldn't move so suddenly! But the words were only in Aiz's mind, and by the time she could form them on her lips, it was too late.

"———————————Hngh?!"

He curled in on himself as his entire body cried out in agony.

And then he began groaning in front of Aiz, like some kind of crazed, pained rabbit.

Aiz hesitated for a few moments, watching the boy suffer, before finally opening her mouth with a look of resolve.

"Are you all right?"

Bell flinched.

The body that had been writhing in such horrible agony froze.

He was still a moment, then raised his head with a snap.

Gold met rubellite as their gazes locked, the two of them close enough to touch.

"I...erm...uh..."

"...Everything okay?"

What looked like a thousand different expressions ran across Bell's face as he took in the sight of Aiz sitting next to him.

Her brows were furrowed, pity coloring her features at the boy's distressed state.

Maybe he hit his head really hard. She couldn't help but worry.

Bell, on the other hand, was oblivious to Aiz's anxiety as his actions grew more and more peculiar, until finally he grasped his current situation. He gulped.

The color of his face changed quickly after that, almost as if he had suddenly realized that the person he'd begged in his half-comatose state had been none other than Aiz. The fingers he'd dug into Aiz's boot began to tremble as his face paled, then flushed red before turning white again.

"Wh-why are you…here…?"

"We stopped here…on the way back from our expedition…" Aiz explained with a slight pause at the boy's trembling half question, relaying her familia's current situation.

Bell fidgeted as he took in the information, and his eyes refused to stay on Aiz.

All of a sudden, he jerked forward.

"My…! My friends, are they—?!" he started. However, the moment he pressed his hand down on the bed to rise, his elbow crumpled.

His wounded, fatigued body was still incapable of sudden movement, no matter what he intended, and he ended up pitching forward.

Aiz reacted instinctively as she watched the boy fall.

Coming forward with her arms outstretched, she caught him with a cushiony *bwoof!*

"…"

"…"

Aiz's hands were on Bell's shoulders. His face, on the other hand, had settled quite comfortably between Aiz's breasts.

His mouth, his nose, his eyes—everything was enveloped by her chest and silver armor.

They made for a lovely shock absorber, and there was no way it

could have hurt. Yet for some reason, Bell remained completely frozen there.

Did he bump his nose?

She sat there worrying at the white mop that was the back of his head until he shot away from her with a mighty jolt.

"I'm so sorry!!"

He launched himself so far away his back traced an uncanny curve while his face adopted the color of a ripened apple.

In fact, he flew so far that his head collided neatly with the floor, which Aiz had tried to warn him about, but she had been a bit too late. Pain shot through the boy's body, and he writhed with an inaudible scream.

Aiz became so flustered that she couldn't respond at all as Bell doubled over with his hands clutching at his stomach, until—

"—Ah. Welf."

The boy's rubellite eyes suddenly noticed his companion lying next to him.

Fighting through the pain, he managed to push himself up into a sitting position to inspect the human boy and prum girl still sleeping soundly, as he'd been doing only a few moments ago. When he saw they were alive and well, he let his muscles relax and dropped back to the floor.

"They'll be all right…Riveria and the others healed them," Aiz explained as she scooted toward the relieved boy. "His injuries were bad, but…you got really hurt, too…" she added, peering at the smith boy's leg before reaching a sympathetic hand toward Bell's forehead.

Her fingers gently combed his white bangs, stroking his forehead through a bandage of gauze like a sister caring for her younger brother.

The touch of her slender fingers produced a brilliant flush on Bell's face.

Aiz cocked her head curiously.

"Are you all right?"

Which only served to redden his face further as the blush spread to his ears and neck.

As strange as she found this reaction, however, she didn't stop.

"Th-thank you...for saving me...really..." Bell stuttered, finally managing to pull himself away from Aiz's touch.

"Of course." She shook her head, saying, *There's no need to thank me* in her heart as a tiny smile formed on her lips. The boy almost looked a little embarrassed.

The two simply stared at each other for a few moments before Aiz gently turned to face the tent's entrance.

"Do you think you can move now?"

"I...I think...so..."

"I'm supposed to report to Finn...I mean, to our captain, about your condition. Do you think you could come with me?"

Bell nodded in response, and Aiz rose to her feet. Her thoughts still lingering on the boy's injuries, she extended a hand to help him walk.

"I-I'm fine!" he stammered, pulling his hand away. He wasn't about to let himself turn any redder than he already had.

While the boy rose to his feet unassisted, Aiz found herself frozen to the spot, hand still outstretched.

I...I touched him too much, didn't I...?

His forehead. His bangs.

Maybe he didn't like it?

Regret colored her thoughts as she recalled the way her hand had moved almost involuntarily toward the fur of that tiny rabbit. She couldn't help but think of her own patron deity, Loki, and the way she constantly flung herself at Aiz and Tiona while denying any ulterior motives. *"This ain't sexual harassment!"*

Her shoulders dropped with a tangible gloominess.

"I-it's not what you think, Miss Aiz. I...It's like a man's sense of honor? I-I mean..." Bell began furtively, stumbling over his words, but he was ultimately unable to finish due to the pain.

In the end, he could get to his feet on his own, and the two of them made their way through the exit to the camp outside.

"Whoa..." Bell seemed a bit in awe as he took in the sight of *Loki Familia's* base camp.

Tent after tent was interspersed with a multitude of cargo and supplies. Aiz felt a smile form on her lips as she watched him look around in curious excitement…though at the same time, the other members of *Loki Familia* scrutinized him with suspicious unease.

The gazes aimed their way were pointed, almost accusatory.

"…?"

Is something wrong? Aiz thought to herself, finding all of this incredibly strange as, next to her, the target of those glares began to pale.

The beautiful top-tier adventurer had no idea that she—along with her heroic, unfaltering service for the boy—could have anything to do with this unwelcoming atmosphere.

"*What?!* Little Argonaut is *here?!*"

Tiona's voice arose with a clamor from a small corner of the camp.

"A-Argonaut…?" Lefiya faltered, shocked by Tiona's sudden shout. She'd been in the middle of explaining the current situation—and Bell Cranell's presence in the camp—to the two Amazonian sisters.

It was already "noontime" in the Dungeon.

Since yesterday, the two Amazons had busied themselves caring for their poison-afflicted companions while also gathering food and water for the group. Just now, however, they'd left to exterminate a swarm of monsters a short distance from camp, and while they had previously heard about the battered trio of adventurers found near the floor's exit, they'd yet to learn the full story.

Normally, they received the news from Aiz, but the swordswoman had been holed up in a tent with the adventurers ever since Riveria and the others had finished their healing procedures. Someone needed to watch over them, after all, and as the white-haired boy was an acquaintance of Aiz's, she seemed like the best one for the job—Riveria's recommendation had also contributed greatly, as the high elf had noticed Aiz's complete inability to settle down after the boy's arrival.

"Y'hear that, Tione? Little Argonaut! The Little Argonaut! Can you believe he's already made it this far? That fight of his was, like, yesterday!"

"Do you have to keep shouting like that? I heard the first time! And what's with that stupid nickname you've given him...?"

"Hee-hee-hee, from the fairy tale, silly! Fits him perfectly, don'tcha think?" Tiona grinned wide, her cheeks flushed.

Tione, however, looked exasperated. "You're a moron."

The younger of the two sisters began flailing around with her giant double-bladed sword, Urga, eliciting a startled look of confusion from Lefiya and an ever-so-fleeting smile from Tione.

"True, though...It really does get your blood pumping just knowing he's here," the older girl mused as a truly Amazonian grin of excitement crept across her face.

"Where's he at anyway, huh, Lefiya? Where's our Little Argonaut?"

"Seems he's in some kind of meeting with the captain..." Lefiya explained somewhat sullenly.

Tiona, in direct contrast, let out an exuberant "Let's go see him when he's done!"

Bidding farewell to Lefiya, the twins returned to their tent to store their weapons.

"First Miss Aiz...now Miss Tiona and Miss Tione, too...?" Lefiya grumbled, her lips turned downward in a disgruntled pout. The excitement around this boy never seemed to end, and now he'd even forced his way right into their camp...

It almost felt as if she'd had her beloved older sisters stolen right out from under her.

Puffing up her cheeks, she resumed attending to the camp duties she'd been assigned.

"Who in the world do you think that white-haired human is, huh, Mister Raul?"

"Yeah, to have Miss Aiz looking after him personally like that... He must be an upper-class adventurer, yeah? But I've never seen or heard of him!"

"How am I supposed to know? Guys, relax already, geez..."

From Lefiya's point of view, it didn't seem as if the rest of the camp was taking the boy's presence too kindly, either. Most of the men who had collected around Raul, for instance, seemed especially moody.

"And what was he thinkin', bringing people from other familias here, yeah?" The complaints continued, creating a spiteful air over the camp. Everyone except Tsubaki and her smiths seemed no happier about that young *Hephaistos Familia* smith than they were about the white-haired human.

"White-haired brat!" "Stealing our Miss Aiz...!" "He makes me so mad!" "She's never taken care of any of us like that...!" "He doesn't know a damn thing!" "Our beautiful Sword Princess is supposed to watch over *us* from the sidelines!"

One after another, they announced their opinions with no subtlety.

Though they normally kept a vague distance between themselves and the gorgeous, otherworldly swordswoman as a sign of humility, they held nothing but admiration and respect for their golden-haired, golden-eyed Sword Princess.

Surrounded by all the negativity directed at the mysterious white rabbit, Lefiya took the opportunity to ask everyone exactly how they felt.

"What about you all? How do you feel about the situation?" she asked, questioning the other girls tasked with cooking duty.

Aki, Narfi, and Leene exchanged looks with one another as they bustled about the crates of supplies, chopping mushrooms and herbs, and boiled the water they'd collected from the pool for the soup.

"Well, I mean, they're adventurers, too, right? So we kinda have to help 'em, yeah?" Aki laid her thoughts out before Narfi continued.

"Imagine how guilty we would feel if we simply abandoned them there."

The two Level-4, second-tier adventurers exchanged wry smiles.

"And that one boy seems to be a friend of Miss Aiz's..." Leene, this time, adjusted her glasses nervously. She'd been given a break from her healing duties and was currently helping the others cook.

Hearing this, Lefiya couldn't help the pout that formed on her lips.

"Though I do find it odd..." Leene continued.

"Odd?"

"I would have thought that Mister Raul would feel the same as the other men…" She glanced toward a circle of lower-level adventurers a short distance away, a sullen Raul at the center of the ring of grievances.

"Well, Raul…maybe you could say that he has a lot of life experience. It's more like he doesn't have the time to be bothering with stuff like that," Narfi added somewhat sardonically as she smirked at the young man a few years her senior, who was being overwhelmed by the onslaught of his peers (*"Stop it, guuuys…"*).

"…Raul and I joined around the same time." Aki glanced up from stirring the big pot of soup over the fire. "By the time we did, that girl…Aiz was already a Level Two."

"Y-you mean that rumor? Of her breaking the record for fastest level-up at the age of eight?"

"Indeed. That tiny little girl…or should I say toddler? She could move like the wind, mincing monsters in the blink of an eye with her sword." Aki half chuckled into the soup as her wooden spoon stirred it around and around. Leene, too, nodded as though remembering the spectacle herself.

"Now, Raul—that scared the crap outta him. Started calling her 'Miss Aiz.' Can you imagine? I mean, sure, I respected her, too, but I just didn't see the sort of 'idol' Loki always made her out to be. So I just watched her…as she got bigger and bigger."

Aki examined her companion, who was still flailing his arms wearily in the middle of the circle.

"Aiz was a monster back then. Much more so than now…Even I can see the difference."

Narfi, Leene, and Lefiya, none of whom had been in the familia as long as Aki, gave tiny gulps. They knew the current Aiz well enough already.

"So it'll be fine, Lefiya."

"Huh?"

"Since you, Tiona, and Tione joined the familia, Aiz has mellowed out quite a bit. She actually smiles now."

It had been three years, now, since Lefiya had joined *Loki Familia*. By the time Lefiya, a Level-2 honors student fresh out of the

© Kiyotaka Haimura

Education District, had passed through the gate to Twilight Manor, Aiz already had Tiona and Tione to pull her out of her shell.

She didn't need to worry, and she didn't need to be jealous, either—that was what the catgirl adventurer was trying to tell her with a grin. And when Lefiya realized she'd been read like a book, her face began to heat up like an oven.

She promptly launched herself into her work to hide her shame, peeling fruit to throw into the pot as Narfi and Leene giggled discreetly.

R-right! Aiz and the rest of us have a deep bond! One that no random stranger can just push his way into!

Lefiya's mood brightened considerably after Aki's reassurance, a smile rising to her face as she continued her cooking duties.

The smile, however, gradually morphed the longer she peeled.

But didn't Miss Aiz say that boy was only a Level 1 before the expedition...? A complete nobody from an unknown familia?

The boy's face flashed through her head, as well as the complete disgrace he'd made of himself running away from her in the streets of Orario.

How on earth had he made it all the way here to the eighteenth floor in such a short period of time...?

It was true he'd received special training from Aiz the same as she had, but...

She couldn't hold in the multitude of feelings flooding her mind as she thought of that boy she'd so one-sidedly deemed her rival.

Eventually, the group of girls finished preparing dinner.

Lefiya was strolling about the camp in hopes of helping out with another set of duties, when she caught a glimpse of Aiz emerging from the main tent.

She brightened instantly...until she saw that white-haired boy exit behind her. In response, she quickly assumed an air of disinterest. He looked nervous, the distrusting gazes of everyone in camp leading him to stick to Aiz's back like glue, much like a frightened rabbit.

Try as she might to act like nothing was wrong, the more Lefiya looked at them, the more her insides churned.

Watching other familia members toss out greetings in Aiz's direction, she abruptly changed her own course, cutting a beeline toward the pair.

"—Thank you for all your hard work, Miss Aiz!"

"Same to you, Lefiya."

She passed by Aiz with a smile—before her path took her right by the boy at her rear.

Her pleasant demeanor vanished in an instant as she directed an intense glare at him.

"Eek!" The mage's menacing expression drew a tiny squeak from the boy.

His face paled in fear.

Her azure eyes met his rubellite ones as her elegant eyes pierced him, slender elven ears twitching.

Their fated meeting by the city walls, their grand game of cat and mouse.

The boy's face quivered as though he did, indeed, remember her—the beautiful fairy who'd hounded him through the city streets.

If you do anything, anything to Miss Aiz, you'll regret the day you were born...!

Wh-whaaaaaa...?!

The silent, vehement exchange passed between them without a word.

In that single moment, that single glance, she communicated everything she wanted to say.

And then it was over, Lefiya continuing her walk and leaving the boy drenched in a cold, trembling sweat. Her warning properly conveyed, she gave a slight *harrumph* before moving on.

Still huffing and puffing, she glanced back once she was a good distance away to see the boy still practically latched onto Aiz's backside.

She was observing him as well as making sure he wouldn't do anything untoward.

And she continued to do so, checking in on them again and again as she went about her work, the same as her equally disobliging companions.

As she intensely focused on that sight in her peripheral vision—

"Ha-*ha*! It really is Little Argonaut!"

—a bright, cheery voice rang out.

It was none other than Tiona, wearing a grand smile.

She dashed over toward Aiz and Bell, who were currently engaged in some sort of conversation, shortly followed by her sister, Tione.

"I'd heard you got lugged into camp, but I didn't realize you were awake! Great!"

Her booming voice could be heard all throughout camp, and her pure joy was perceptible to everyone. Bell, however, found himself immediately flustered by the euphoric girl headed straight toward him. Lefiya, too, felt her mood instantly plummet as she watched.

It seemed they were going to introduce themselves to the boy, the oh-so-naive and innocent Tiona and her seemingly interested sister, Tione.

But the sight of the twin beauties rushing toward him, bantering with him, only made the boy's face redden like a tomato.

Their robust tanned skin, their exposed bellies, their slender hips, and perky chests—he was being seduced by the fearsome bodies of the Amazons!

With Aiz in the mix, currently cocking her head to the side curiously, it made for three beautiful women, all there waiting on him hand and foot.

Lefiya had just warned him about this!!

Don't get carried away.

Don't get so damn carried away.

Don't get soooooo carried away!

PLEASE DON'T GET CARRIED AWAAAAAAAAAY...!!

The words repeated themselves like a spell in Lefiya's soul, her resentment matching those of the nearby male demi-humans.

All around her those malicious stares gathered on the sight like a murderous barrage aimed at a dragon.

The boy must have felt it, turning white as a sheet beneath the withering glares of Lefiya and her male companions.

"I-I have to...go check on my friends!" he shouted before turning tail and fleeing what felt like a real threat to his life. He practically dived back into the tent he'd been allocated, caring little for pretense.

"Oh dear. He left!" Lefiya mused half-delightedly and half-regretfully, unable to resist, upon the boy's forced flight before dashing over to where Aiz, Tiona, and Tione still stood side by side.

"I-I, erm…! I-I just wanted to ask, but…you were all fussing over that human so much. Did something happen between you and that adventurer?" she asked, despite already knowing his connection to Aiz, at least.

It was Tiona's and Tione's overwhelming interest in the boy, however, that had her scratching her head, as she couldn't think of a time when the three would have crossed paths. All she had to go on was Finn's mention of his name down on the fifty-ninth floor. She needed to know.

Tiona and Tione glanced at each other, looking very much like two mirror images.

"Something happened, all right…" Tione began with a wry smile.

"Yeah, a miracle!" Tiona continued next to her, unable to hold back her excited shout. "He took down a minotaur at Level One!"

"All by himself, too."

Lefiya stopped short. Then she looked to Aiz…

…who only nodded in affirmation.

"He…he…he…"

But Lefiya couldn't find the words.

"—These brave adventurers were willing to give up their own lives to save those of their companions in order to reach this eighteenth floor. While I'm not asking you to be their best friends, I do ask that you show them at least a shred of respect. We're all adventurers down here, after all…Now then, shall we get back to the matter at hand?" Finn's voice cut through the darkness of the forest around them.

The large circle of adventurers surrounding the campfire-like mound of magic stones raised their glasses.

"Cheers!"

Thus, the meager feast began.

They were seated in the large, open space at the base camp's center. "Night" had settled over the Dungeon; the crystals coating the ceiling far above their branch-sheltered camp were silent.

It was a dinner similar to the one from a night prior, only this time, Aiz had brought Bell and his fellow adventurers, since the young smith and prum girl had recovered to the point where they could walk.

Finn's speech acted more as an unsaid warning to the group—that they should do their best to avoid any disputes—and the men who'd been harboring their resentment all day could only bow their heads in shame. Self-respect as upper-class adventurers and a need to keep face as the largest familia in Orario both contributed to a decidedly warmer reception of Bell.

After their self-admonition, they were able to enjoy the evening meal wholeheartedly.

And so *Loki Familia*, together with the small group of *Hephaistos Familia* smiths, partook in food and drink beneath the watchful gaze of the fluttering Trickster flag. Supper was mushrooms seasoned with what little salt they had left and a soup of sour-tasting fruits, all of which they devoured before washing it down with cool, clean river water that had been chilled with ice magics. Every bit of the meal permeated their fatigued, expedition-weary bodies.

It had taken considerable ingenuity to craft such a supper from the tiny amount of supplies they had left, but the smiles blooming on faces all throughout the circle were worth it.

"…"

That is, except for the face of a certain elven mage, who was currently sitting silently by herself and eating neither soup nor fruits as the cheerful voices echoed around her.

Her eyes were fixated on the small group of adventurers seated a short distance away—a group that consisted of Aiz, Bell, and his two companions.

She watched as the boy took a piece of offered Honey Cloud, eyeing it curiously, taking a tiny nibble, then immediately stiffening, as though he was holding in a sudden urge to vomit.

He took down a minotaur at Level 1...

She couldn't think about anything but what Tiona and Tione had told her earlier. She couldn't get Bell out of her head. It was impossible to ignore it.

Lefiya's mastery of Concurrent Casting under Aiz's and the others' tutelage was impressive enough...but now her opponent had gone and defeated an enormous, Level-2-category monster all on his own. And a minotaur, of all things! A symbol of sheer power and endurance. Challenging one head-on was a trying task even for a third-tier adventurer.

To think that a Level 1 could do such a thing was beyond irritating, and Lefiya felt herself losing control of her rancor again.

"Those youngsters are certainly havin' a good time in spite of it all." Opposite Lefiya's building rage, Gareth sat stroking his long beard from atop the seats of honor reserved for *Loki Familia*'s elites.

"They are, indeed," Finn responded with a laugh.

Right across from them in their own corner of the circle sat Aiz, Bell, and his companions, the four of them in high spirits as they went about their meal. Apparently, a fight for the fruits had broken out.

The prum girl was red-faced, kicking the back of the young smith as she let out squeals of frustration. The smith, on the other hand, had made clean work of the piece of Honey Cloud in question, the cotton-like fruit nowhere to be found. Bell's face twitched as he watched the argument play out, while Aiz simply stared on in bewilderment.

The entertaining spectacle was enough to draw snickering out of not only the women but the entire familia.

"Mmph—Tione! Fwe sh—nngulp!—we should go join Little Argonaut!"

"Don't talk with your mouth full! The food's not going anywhere, yeah? And I'd rather not see it after it goes into that mouth of yours! You are such a child, ugh! Ah! Captain! Would you like something to drink?"

"Hm? Ah, yes. Thank you."

But in the end, *Loki Familia* would not be beaten when it came to being lively.

Already, Tiona was on her umpteenth bowl of soup, and once Tione had finished admonishing her, the younger sister sidled up next to Finn with an alluring voice.

She refilled the prum captain's cup from a calabash-shaped fruit known as the gourd berry. Cutting away the thick-skinned upper tip and pressing on the body of the fruit would squeeze out its jelly-like red flesh. The flesh itself started sour and grew sweeter the more it ripened. If left for too long, the fruit turned bitter. That taste was a sign of fermentation—the alcohol it produced was cherished for its ability to soothe the tongues and throats of upper-class adventurers who were stuck in the Dungeon but longed for the ale of the surface.

Even Riveria, who normally steered clear of all alcohol, was known to partake in the drink of the gourd berry from time to time.

Now, too, the high-elf queen was being recommended it by the other elves in the familia, and she drank the Dungeon fruit spirit (though not to become intoxicated, of course) with a smile on her face.

"M-Miss Tsubaki! Gimme a break, here! I-isn't this that crazy dwarf liquor...?!"

"Man up, you puppy! It's only a little dwarven fire drink, yeah? I just felt like opening up a bottle!" Tsubaki responded, undeterred, as she poured Raul a glass of the alcohol she'd traded for in Rivira.

Raul, in turn, flushed a brilliant red all the way to his ears, drunk in an instant thanks to that bottle and its dwarven insignia.

"Hmph. No fun! Oi, Gareth! Show me that liver of steel!" Tsubaki moved on as Raul passed out on the ground, her own cheeks mildly pink.

"As much as I'd like to join ye, lass...I have me position to consider. Be glad t'join ye for one back on the surface," Gareth explained before noticing the piercing gaze aimed at him from just beside the leaping flames. "...Riveria! No need fer those steely eyes. I know, I know!"

The humorous exchange was enough to make *Loki Familia*'s lower-level members burst into laughter.

The mood was relaxed, and everyone was hanging loose now that their expedition was close to completion.

It was a moment of celebration, a toast to a battle hard-won, back-dropped by nightfall's dark forest—a scene that wouldn't look out of place in a picture book. The boy with white hair gazed out over the revelry, lips relaxing into a smile as he eyed the cheerful circle of adventurers.

It was even more spirited than the night before.

"Tsubaki. I'd heard one of your familia's smiths was among those brought to camp...Would it be that young man over there?" Riveria asked as she threw a watchful glance toward the guards they had surveying the perimeter.

"No mistake about it! Hee-hee...Now that he's up and at 'em, it's high time I got over there and pestered him a little!" Tsubaki exclaimed, taking one look at the red-haired boy in question before shooting to her feet with a wide grin. Together with the other high smiths (and a bottle of liquor), she made a beeline for Bell's group.

The boy himself gave a sudden *urk*, brows knitting together like a tightly wound hemp basket.

"What's with the face, Welfy? And here I came all the way over here to see if ya were okay!"

"Don't gimme that! I can smell the alcohol on your breath from a mile away!"

"What were ya thinking, though, huh? Comin' all the way down here to the eighteenth floor in a party with these other folks?" she continued unfazed, ignoring the boy's blatant hostility at her drunken state. As her junior smith gritted his teeth and growled ("Why you...!"), she caught a glance of the white-haired boy sitting next to him.

Tsubaki stared. In fact, she looked at him so long that the boy grew rather uncomfortable, fidgeting restlessly.

"Oh?"

She looked back and forth between Aiz and the boy until, finally, she clapped her hands together as if reaching some sort of realization.

"Oh, I know who you are! You're that Crell Banell fella!!" she bellowed excitedly, remembering the alleged "amazing adventurer" they'd run into on their way to the eighteenth floor whom Tiona had mentioned earlier during their descent into the Dungeon.

"I-I think you have me confused with somebody else," Bell replied, a drop of sweat running down his temple.

However, Tsubaki didn't pay much attention to the boy's denial. Instead, the half-dwarf master smith grabbed his hand with a sturdy grip and gave it a bone-cracking shake along with a smile.

"They call me Tsubaki!"

Meanwhile, the bearer of erroneous info herself was just finishing up her meal. "I'm dooone!" she shouted before shifting her attention away without so much as wiping her mouth. "Little Arrrgonaaaut!" she shouted before she and Tione rose to their feet and leaped toward Bell and his companions.

In the midst of all the excitement, a certain sullen elf finally raised her voice. "...Erm, Lady Riveria? Captain?" Lefiya neared the group of familia elites. "I was just wondering if...if you, too, witnessed Bell Cranell defeating a minotaur?"

Gareth, Riveria, and Finn exchanged glances before the latter two nodded.

"We did."

"'Fraid I missed it, lass. As ye can probably remember, I was with ye and the others in the rearguard while that young'un was workin' his miracle on the ninth floor..." Gareth responded with a regretful stroke of his beard.

"Finn and I, however, were there to observe it."

"As were Aiz, Bete, Tiona, and Tione."

Riveria and Finn countered respectively, both of them glancing in Bell's direction.

"I just...Did he really, really take down that beast all by himself? Without any help from you or Miss Aiz?"

"He did. Had he not, he'd not be with us today," Finn responded with a laugh.

"As a matter of fact, Aiz herself stopped us from helping him," Riveria continued somewhat playfully, her eyes closed.

It was quite the spectacle, both of them confirmed wholeheartedly, voices steeped in admiration.

Lefiya felt an emotion that could only be described as "intense anguish" filling her up from the inside out upon confirmation of her rival's feat.

I was not able to take on a minotaur single-handedly until I'd reached Level 3…

She knew it was like comparing apples and oranges. That mages were different from adventurers. That those on the back line were different from those on the front line.

But, all the same, she couldn't stop herself, simply because she and Bell Cranell were both protégés of her beloved Aiz.

"Nnngh," she grumbled as she stood before her three superiors.

She peered at Bell, who in the brief moment she'd been looking away, had once again garnered the attention of Aiz, Tiona, and Tione. All of them had encircled him with excited, inquisitive questions about his earlier achievement, and Lefiya even heard them say, "How in the world did you get all your abilities to S?!" as the boy sat there fidgeting awkwardly. Finn and the others, too, turned their gazes toward the scene, but while they exchanged brief sighs, they did nothing to intervene.

H-he's at it again…!!

Her intense anguish quickly combined with flames of rage, and she immediately charged toward the boy, who had broken out in a cold sweat.

"—Nnnghahh?!"

"?!"

It was at that moment—

—the scream of what seemed to be a young girl reached the camp.

There was a flurry of activity from the direction of the perimeter guards, when the white-haired boy suddenly rose to his feet and took off with nothing but a succinct "Excuse me for a moment!" The others were quick to follow—the prum girl, the smith boy, then Aiz, Tiona, and Tione, as well.

The whole camp was instantly alight with excitement.

It would seem the number of unexpected guests was about to rise yet again.

FLIP SIDE OF THE COMPROMISE

Гэта казка іншага сям'і.

Задняя частка пасёлка

"So sorry for dropping by unannounced like this, but consider my surprise. *Loki Familia*...saving Bell of all people. Color me shocked!" The gentlemanly god smiled coyly as he spoke to them with deliciously clear enunciation.

There was an almost collective sigh from his followers behind him. The passing visitors were gathered in *Loki Familia*'s main tent for a meeting with Finn and the other elites.

The feminine scream that had pierced the air of the camp during their feast had been none other than Bell Cranell's patron deity, Hestia, on her way down from the seventeenth floor.

She had intentionally descended into the Dungeon in an attempt to save her dear follower and his companions—willfully defying the statutes set by the Guild—only to find herself suddenly unable to escape. Even for Finn and Gareth, who'd been adventurers of Orario for a long time, this was a first, and seeing her within the Dungeon's confines was enough for their smiles to turn very troubled.

It hadn't been just Hestia, though, as evidenced by the well-mannered god standing before them now together with his followers and other adventurers.

"Pardon me, God Hermes, while I try to wrap my head around this, but...you're saying that you came all the way down here to the eighteenth floor...to save Bell Cranell and his party?"

"You would be most correct, my dear Braver. As part of a request from Hestia. I even have the official quest form here, see?" Hermes replied as *Loki Familia*'s leaders, Finn, Riveria, and Gareth, looked on.

Joining them in the main tent were the other *Loki Familia* elites—except Bete—as well as non-elite Raul (who would report the details of the meeting later to Lefiya and everyone else still currently cleaning up the dinner area).

Aiz and the others watched on as Hermes pulled out the aforementioned request form. On the parchment, the approving seal of the Guild, as well as the reward of four hundred thousand valis, was clearly present.

Hey there.

…Hello.

From behind Hermes, his follower Asfi greeted her with a smile so slight only Aiz would notice it. Aiz had fought alongside the *Hermes Familia* captain, Asfi Al Andromeda, during the incident in the twenty-fourth-floor pantry. Their short time in the same party made them what other adventurers referred to as "floor buddies."

Responding to the aqua-blue-eyed girl, Aiz returned the smile with one of her own.

"Though I am highly curious as to why your party's simply camped out here on the eighteenth floor…let's keep to the matter at hand, shall we?" Hermes continued, acting as the rescue party's ambassador.

Hestia, on the other hand, had been moved to the tent Bell was currently borrowing. Though Aiz was curious about the apparent discord she sensed between Bell's goddess and the adventurers dressed in Far Eastern garb, she felt her duty as one of the familia's elites was to hear out the "part explanation, part negotiation" Hermes had promised in his meeting.

"We'd like permission to stay here. With all of you. Also, if it's at all possible, we were hoping to join you on your return to the surface."

"So you're not killed along the way?" Finn mused.

Hermes nodded with a little grin. "Glad we're both on the same page."

Bell and his companions had originally fled to the eighteenth floor in hopes of banding together with higher-class adventurers in order to escape the danger zone of the middle levels. Now Hermes aimed to do the same. Though his rescue party didn't lack in combat power, there wasn't much meaning in taking unnecessary risks. After all, Goliath still prowled the seventeenth floor.

Allowing *Loki Familia* to act as a spear carving its way toward the surface and simply following in their wake was the safest choice by far.

"We were in such a hurry to get down here and rescue Bell that we didn't think about bringing camping provisions. Of course, we could always stay in that cesspool they call the 'Rogue Town'…"

"And of couuuurse Little Argonaut and his friends would have a terrible time there," Tiona grumbled softly, hands laced behind her head.

"Quiet," Tione said as she jabbed her sister with her elbow.

"Food-wise, we'll figure something out ourselves. If our presence should lead to any sort of incurred expenses, my familia will foot the bill upon arrival on the surface. Of course, if you'd so wish it, I can also provide some sort of remuneration."

"Yer bein' rather generous for a man who's merely carryin' out a request."

"Ha-ha, well, I did also have Hephaistos come to me right before I left, asking me to help out her little Welf, you know?"

This god's really good at negotiating.

Aiz thought this to herself about Asfi's patron deity as she watched him. Expressing both his true motives and polite regard for the other party, then pressing with just enough awareness of the situation to ensure they would be disinclined to refuse. He knew that *Loki Familia* couldn't possibly abandon a member of an allied familia. Hearing this, even Gareth couldn't help but sigh.

"I do apologize for any trouble this may cause you, as I know that you must be tired after your expedition…but I hope you'll consider it."

Hermes…He was famous for his tendency to aid not only random strangers on the road but merchants, as well. He was also a god known for falsifying the levels of followers in his neutral familia. His skill with words was of an entirely different variety compared to Loki.

As Aiz stood there now observing this deity, having just returned from the trip he'd taken immediately following Denatus some ten days ago, she couldn't help but think him quite shrewd.

"Lord Hermes, if you would, I don't care much for needless haggling. So long as you and your followers don't cause any sort of trouble around here, you're welcome to stay and leave with us for the surface. After all, it would be cruel of us to simply abandon those we've already taken under our wing."

"Oh, you are too kind, too kind! You have my utmost thanks."

Finn gave in to Hermes's request. He hadn't exactly left them with much choice, which had undoubtedly been the god's intention.

Once the deal had been struck, Finn went on to explain their current situation—the poison-vermis attack and their stopover here on the eighteenth floor, all of which Hermes took in with an understanding "I see..." Finn continued by relaying their estimated time of departure and allocating the newcomers tents for the night, keeping the conversation rolling.

"Oh dear, I'd almost forgotten! Though I may be a bit late, congratulations on a successful return from your expedition...at least, I assume it's a successful return?"

Hermes's comment came right as the discussion was wrapping up, the god's characteristic smile back on his face.

"Thank you. We are returning with zero casualties."

"Amazing! I should have expected no less from *Loki Familia*," Hermes began, excitement creeping into his voice, before continuing. "Then I do have to wonder...What might you have found down on the fifty-ninth floor, hm?" he mused, clearly probing. While the smile on his lips never faltered, his thin, bow-like eyes widened eagerly.

Those all-seeing eyes seemed to stare straight through them, and Aiz couldn't help but give a little start. Even Tiona's and Tione's faces instantly stiffened, though of the group, only Raul showed any obvious outward signs of discomfort.

Finn's, Riveria's, and Gareth's composure, however, never cracked.

"We are followers of Loki. We have no duty to disclose familia matters to gods with questionable intentions." Riveria was the first to speak, one eye closed as she shot Hermes down.

Behind Hermes, Asfi reacted to the sudden tense atmosphere with the aura of someone who had gone through much hardship, one hand gently cradling her abdomen.

"Right you are. I do apologize. It's simply that you're the first ones to tread on such ground since Zeus's party did so long ago. The entire city is watching you, so I'll admit I was a bit curious myself," Hermes responded, unfazed, seemingly aloof toward the goings-on of the city and its people. "Ah, right. Have you heard that I'm now in an alliance with Loki and Dionysus?"

"!"

"The three of us have come together as victims of the same crimes. To take a stand against those vibrantly colored monsters and the remnants of the Evils," he continued with a blasé attitude as Aiz and the others attempted to digest the latest piece of surprising news.

Finn, however, remained as cool as ever. "I'm afraid we'll have to confirm this with our own goddess before we can fully believe you, Lord Hermes."

"Of course, of course! In that case, feel free to ignore what I'm about to tell you now, hm?" Hermes began before continuing. "Though you may have already noticed, Braver, Finn Deimne... somewhere aboveground, there is another entrance into this mighty Dungeon besides the one found in Babel. That's the conclusion your goddess and I came to."

The gulps were almost audible this time.

Even the gazes of Riveria and Gareth hardened.

"Which is why we were hoping...for you to perform a systematic search all throughout Orario and its periphery upon your return to the surface." Hermes's orange eyes narrowed, his gaze never leaving that of the tiny, motionless familia captain in front of him.

After an extended pause, he turned away.

"Consider it compensation for our lodging, small as it may be. Do take care of it, hm?" he added before making his way out of the tent.

Asfi was quick to follow, giving a short bow before leaving the group, and the tent, in silence.

"C-Captain...?" Raul finally uttered. Hermes's offhanded information was still hanging over their heads.

The others responded by turning their gazes toward their small prum leader, faces a varied mixture of emotions. Finn brought his right hand to his mouth, giving his thumb a little lick.

"Though I somehow expected this...it seems we're not going to be getting much rest once we return home," he sighed with a shake of his head.

"This thing is big...very big..."

The quiet murmur resonated louder than expected within the large tent.

Lefiya and the others turned toward Tione anxiously, the Amazon currently standing near the tent's far edge.

Immediately after their meeting with Hermes had ended, they'd rounded up everyone who'd taken part in the fifty-ninth-floor raid, and they'd all congregated here, in one of *Loki Familia*'s female tents. Lefiya and the other Level-4 second-battalion members, and even Aki, were all present. Raul and the men, however, were still outside giving orders, and Aiz and Riveria were nowhere to be found.

"Y'know, uh...as honored as I feel to be here...is it really okay? I mean, I'm totally an outsider," Tsubaki piped up from within the women-only tent.

"It's fine. You were there on the fifty-ninth floor, too, so you already know everything...Besides, it'd be best to hear opinions from everyone," Tione responded with a drop of her shoulders.

The half-dwarf just laughed. "Then let the party begin!"

Since the moment the familia leaders had concluded the meeting, Tione and the others had been racking their brains, trying to come up with an explanation for this string of strange events. They hadn't had much of a chance to discuss things, what with their expedition and other happenings, so it seemed like a good chance to do so after hearing Hermes's info.

"B-but...it just seems impossible, right? For there to be another entrance besides Babel?" Lefiya asked timidly.

"Yeaaah, but this is straight from the gods themselves..." Tiona answered from where she was seated on the floor nearby.

"It does make sense. I mean, how else would somebody be able to lug those giant flowers up to the surface without being seen? Remember during the Monsterphilia and the sewers? If there was only one entrance, we'd have no choice but to suspect the Guild and *Ganesha Familia*," Tione continued, adding in her own two cents.

If there really was a second entrance to the Dungeon besides the great chasm of Babel, it would turn everything they knew on its head. As the scope of the issue grew larger and larger, Lefiya brought her hands to her own head with a tiny moan, unable to wrap her mind around the consequences.

"Though...I'm mostly worried about the thing with Aiz," Tiona began slowly.

The demi-spirit, for instance, what with its strength and its ability to cast magic, was entirely outside the realm of the ordinary. This powerful abnormality could easily surpass even the crimson-haired woman Levis and her other creature friends.

And it seemed Aiz was, in fact, its target.

It had even called her "Aria."

"As I recall, Aiz was the first to recognize that thing as a spirit."

"And she got all weird when she saw it, yeah?"

Alicia and Narfi shared their observations in turn.

Aiz had yet to say anything about what had happened down there, nor did she explain the name the demi-spirit had called her. She'd simply averted her eyes when anyone asked, responding with a quiet "I'm sorry..." before letting the issue die.

"Well, she always has been a bit of an odd duck, if ya ask me," Tsubaki mused, stroking her chin.

"M-Miss Tsubaki!" Lefiya balked.

Tione turned toward Aki. "You've known her the longest, right? You wouldn't happen to know anything, would you?"

"Afraid not. Back then, Aiz was even more of a recluse than she is today...I've asked the bosses about it before, but they just tell me she has her reasons." The black catgirl's shapely eyebrows bowed in apologetic futility.

"Aria, spirits...somehow I can't help but think about that legend *Dungeon Oratoria*." Tiona's eyes rose toward the tent's ceiling in far-off thought.

Tione, however, just frowned. "Then what, are you saying that Aiz is a spirit or something? That legend's centuries old, from back in the Ancient Times, right? To think they'd have any connection is ridiculous."

"I didn't mean it like that..."

"It's true, though, Miss Tiona. Spirits aren't supposed to be able to have children...right?" Lefiya chimed in somewhat skeptically.

The fairy-tale-loving Amazon crossed her arms in deep reflection. "Hmmm...I guess not. Guess it's probably nothing after all..."

Aki and the others exchanged glances.

Almost all the stories they'd been told as children included this "spirit."

But could that spirit of legend really have anything to do with Aiz—some sort of link between humans and demi-humans?

"Puttin' aside kids' stories for now...You do realize there is someone with spirit blood runnin' through their veins, yeah?"

Tsubaki's question hit them like a ton of bricks.

Every head in the tent popped up with a simultaneous "*What?!*"

The *Hephaistos Familia* high smith just laughed.

"I guess that answers that, huh? Why don't I bring him here?"

"...Can I ask why I'm here?" the red-haired boy said incredulously from his position at the center of the tent. He didn't even try to disguise his malcontent, sitting cross-legged on the ground as his eyes took in the wide circle of girls surrounding him.

"As y'all already know, this whelp here is the smith in Bell Cranell's party. He's also one of the grunts in my familia."

The boy Tsubaki had brought back with her was none other than the young smith *Loki Familia* had picked up together with Bell.

"What the hell is going on here, Tsubaki?!" the boy furiously responded, clearly irritated at being dragged here and not afraid to make his displeasure known, even to the captain of his own familia.

Tsubaki, however, ignored him, moving right along even as Lefiya and the other girls looked on in stunned embarrassment.

"This kid's name is Welf Crozzo."

"...Crozzo?"

"Why do I feel like I've heard that name before...?"

Lefiya and Tiona cocked their heads to the side in simultaneous inquisition.

Suddenly, Aki's tail stood straight up. "Wait, you don't mean, like…that cursed magic-sword smith Crozzo, do you?"

"The very same!" Tsubaki responded somewhat triumphantly. "The maker of the invincible swords of legend for the Kingdom of Rakia!…This kid's a descendant of that very smith nobleman."

A shocked silence settled over the tent.

The Crozzo Magic Swords were weapons of legend known not only throughout Orario but the entire world. Originally, magic swords were capable only of producing weak magic in exchange for not requiring chants to cast. Crozzo Magic Swords, however, went far beyond that, producing magic even stronger than the originals, which was why the Kingdom of Rakia of old had long used them in their battles, at least according to the many records left behind.

These weapons were, beyond a doubt, the strongest magic swords in existence, reputed to have lit the sea itself on fire.

And now, Lefiya and the others sat facing a descendant of that smith.

All eyes were glued to the young man with the fiery hair, this Welf Crozzo, although he was glaring daggers at Tsubaki.

"Is…that all true?!"

Someone suddenly shouted.

It was loud enough to make the shoulders of everyone in the tent jump.

"But the Crozzo family, they…they're the ones who burned my home! So many elven tribes have no forest, no village to return to thanks to his family!" screamed the elf Alicia, her face red with rage.

Lefiya found herself at a loss for words. She, too, had heard of the terrible, destructive power of the Crozzo Magic Swords and their use in the Rakian War—stories of battlefields turned to wastelands with nary a blade of grass left. Those flames had reached even the forest of the elves, who were uninvolved in the war but deprived of their homes all the same.

The number of elves who'd lost their villages due to the heedless embers of those magic swords was almost uncountable.

"M-Miss Alicia…"

Compared to Lefiya, who'd grown up under the teachings of both her home and the Education District and had developed a more open-minded way of thinking (or perhaps "naive" was another way of putting it), the truly elven Alicia, whose pride in her people was fiercely intact, looked practically rabid.

The young elf didn't even try to disguise her vehement rage at the smith of those cursed magic swords, who'd brought such destruction to her land. The relatively young Lefiya and Narfi held their breath at the drastic change in the normally calm, composed, and sisterly elf.

Welf, however, merely scowled as the enraged elf leaned forward in unmistakable hatred.

The sudden tension in the tent seemed liable to explode at any moment, and Tiona and Tione stepped forward to quickly bring the situation under control.

"Hold your horses, there, Alicia. Let me finish talking first." Even Tsubaki, rather flabbergasted herself, tried to rein things in. She directed an open palm at the elf, whose green eyes blinked in response. "This kid actually disowned his Crozzo lineage."

"He what…?"

"For reasons I sincerely, honestly, and wholeheartedly can't fathom, little Welfy here loathes every bit of his own heritage. More than that, he despises his own abilities. Y'see, he can forge circles around me when it comes to magic swords, but he won't even touch one to save his life. Talk about wasted talent!"

Considering the fact that the Crozzo line had already fallen into decline and lost its ability to forge the magic swords of the past, hearing that there was someone more talented than a high smith at crafting weapons was shocking to hear for Tione and the others.

"But when he was forced to make 'em, he wound up leaving Rakia and his home behind. So you see, Alicia? He 'n' you may have more in common than ya think!" Tsubaki let out a childish laugh as Alicia simply stared in bewilderment.

The boy in question, on the other hand, only seemed even angrier than before. "Hey! Would ya let a guy speak for himself for once?" he barked in irritation.

"Just tryin' to clear up the confusion was all."

"Yeah, confusion thanks to you and your big mouth!" he shouted with renewed zeal.

Alicia grew visibly uncomfortable as she watched the scene unfold, though Welf continued to ignore her and didn't even bother to spare her a retort. It was almost as if he knew doing so would be completely pointless.

Welf was a true craftsman, untroubled by trivial matters. Or at least that's what Lefiya made of the boy, watching him as she and the others in the tent gave sighs of relief now that the trouble had seemingly passed.

"Goddammit…whatever! Just get to the point and let me outta here," Welf finally implored somewhat desperately, clearly fed up with Tsubaki and her aloofness, showing no signs he cared at all what *Loki Familia* might think of him.

"Then I'm just gonna come right out and ask it, okay?" Tione began. "…Do you or do you not carry the blood of a spirit in your veins?"

"…Just a second here." Welf's eyebrows rose as he immediately looked toward Tsubaki.

"C'mon, it's fine, ain't it? You got nothin' to lose, and these folks here'd really like to know. You can tell 'em!"

Welf simply glared at her, his eyes narrowing in a look that screamed, *How much have you told them?!* Tsubaki responded with a somewhat nonchalant apology.

The boy let out a long, sustained sigh before he nodded.

Identical expressions of shock crossed the faces of everyone in the tent. "…But you better not go spreading rumors! I hate people prying into my business," he warned.

"But…but how could the blood of a spirit…be in a human…?" Lefiya asked in disbelief.

"…I'll skip straight to where it counts. A long, long time ago, back in the Ancient Times, Crozzo the First saved a spirit from a bunch of monsters. In doing so, he ended up badly wounded, and the spirit offered some of her blood as a way of thanks," Welf explained succinctly.

"The spirits' miracle…" Tiona murmured, awestruck.

By sharing her blood with him, the spirit was able to save the man's life. In doing so, she had also shared her magic, giving him the ability to use spirit-borne magic for the rest of his life, imbuing within him her blessings and endowing him with her miraculous powers.

"Then the Crozzo ability to mass-produce those ludicrous swords of his was..." Alicia began.

"I'm sure you can hazard a guess." Welf's shoulders drooped. "A by-product of the blood of our ancestor."

Everyone's questions melted away like cracking ice. Everything made sense. Those swords and their tremendous power, enough to set the very sea on fire, were made possible only thanks to the blessing of an ancient spirit.

This discovery, however, gave rise to even more questions. Why had Crozzo stopped producing his magic swords, for instance? But Welf was in no mood to explain further, replying to all questions with a disgruntled "Haven't I told you enough already?"

Tiona, Tione, Alicia, and the others let out a set of awkward coughs, their faces red. It was true that they may have truly overstepped their boundaries.

—But that didn't eliminate the fact that those with spirit blood could definitely exist.

—Was it possible that Aiz, too...?

While the girls didn't voice such possibilities out loud, the question was plain in their furtive glances around the tent.

Aiz's incredible wind power...Couldn't that be just another by-product of spiritual blood? After all, she had been the first to identify the demi-spirit down on the fifty-ninth floor. And the fact that she'd felt it in her blood reinforced the theory.

If they were to truly continue with this hypothesis, the only question left was how, where, and when Aiz had inherited blood from a spirit.

The tent grew quiet, everyone falling deep into thought.

"You wouldn't happen to know who Aiz's parents are, would you, Aki...?" Tione asked, her voice low.

"Nope. I'd always kinda thought she was just some orphan dropped from the sky..."

"Miss Tiona, in that...legend...did it ever describe the spirit?" Lefiya this time.

"Mmmn...I've never seen the real thing. Both the version of *Dungeon Oratoria* I read as a kid and the one we have back at the manor are just handwritten copies, so who knows what kinda stuff got changed over the years..."

"There's also the possibility that things were edited purposefully..." Alicia mused.

Then Narfi added her own two cents. "Hmm, once we start throwing out ideas, we'll never stop."

"Can I go already?" Welf asked, clearly fed up as the gaggle of girls around him talked quietly among themselves, completely ignoring him.

"Welfy," Tsubaki started, gazing out across the group. "You wouldn't happen to know anything else about the whole 'spiritual connection' thing, would ya? These girls are specially interested in a spirit named Aria who appeared in the old legend."

"How the hell am I supposed to know? It was my great ancestor who had direct contact with that spirit, not me. All I know is what I've been told," he replied sharply, as if trying to distance himself from his past.

"Hnnnnghh," Tsubaki growled, thumping the back of his head impatiently as her chest jostled within its cloth binding. "Man, you're seriously useless when something really matters! This is why I'm always telling you 'It's a decent weapon, but...' or 'This one's a major disappointment'! Remember somethin', goddammit!"

"What the hell is wrong with you? And what do my forging skills have to do with all this anyway?!" Welf spat back, red-faced. He was really angry now. Having suffered one exorbitant request after another and even his pride as a craftsman now wounded, he shoved Tsubaki's hand away with an "I'm done here!"

Absolutely unwilling to stay there even a moment longer, he shouted at them once more.

"If it's the legends you're so interested in, don't ask me! There's someone else who knows a lot more about them than I do!"

"...U-um...why am I...here?"

It was the white-haired boy's turn to be forcefully plopped in the middle of the women-only tent. He sat on his knees, sweat exuding from his every pore as Lefiya's glare of hatred seared his whole body.

"Ho-ho-ho. Bell Cranell. Welfy's done sold you out! You'd best prepare yourself." Tsubaki laughed nefariously, looking more and more like some kind of evil magistrate.

"S-sold out...?!" Bell gulped.

He'd been summoned immediately after Welf had stormed out of the tent in a huff. The smith had been so anxious to remove himself from Tsubaki's vicinity that he'd thought nothing of leading his own party member to the slaughter in his stead—something he may or may not have ended up regretting later.

Sitting there now as part of this *Loki Familia* emergency summons, surrounded entirely by beautiful women (at least one of whom seemed to want him dead), Bell looked very much like a scared little rabbit with nowhere to run. His face had already blanched a lighter shade of white as he fidgeted nervously in his spot.

"We're not gonna bite, so you can calm down, okay? Consider this payment for the room and board, hm? Just answer a few questions for us, and then you can leave," Tione explained, keeping her tone cordial and neighborly in an attempt to calm the fearful, shame-faced, despondent, jittery boy at the center of their circle.

Her smiling face was enough to ease the tension from Bell's shoulders. Meanwhile..."Eh-heh-heh...it's Little Argonaut! It's Little Argonaut!" Tiona was practically rocking back and forth atop her crossed legs as she eagerly eyed Bell. Her eyes glimmered with excitement at the prospect of playing with her new friend. "Hey, hey! I heard you really know a lot about the legends of heroes. Is it true?"

"I, uh...don't really know if it'd be considered a lot, but I did read them often as a child."

This only excited Tiona all the more, and she promptly began testing him.

"Then who's the lady who Sir Garrard saves, huh?"

"Queen Altis..."

"Then, then, where did Giorgio the Dragon Slayer kill the dragon?"

"Lake Sirena..."

© Kiyotaka Haimura

"Then, then, then, what weapon did he use to kill it?"

"A spear-like holy sword...and a maiden's ribbon."

"Awesome!!" Tiona cried out buoyantly when Bell answered every question correctly.

Her face flushed with excitement, she leaned forward in visible anticipation. "Right, then, Little Argonaut! The story of Arcadia—"

"Ahh, put a cork in it already! We have more important things to talk about!" Tione cut in before her sister could steer things any further off track.

Tiona grumbled with a little pout as Aki and Alicia chuckled to themselves at the fairy-tale-loving Amazon's antics.

"Getting back to the topic at hand, do you know anything about a spirit called Aria?" Tione asked, moving right along.

"You mean the great spirit of the *Dungeon Oratoria*? The one closely connected to the life of Albert the Great? That Aria?"

"Yeah, yeah! That one!" Tiona replied happily.

As the legend was one of the world's most well-known fairy tales, its basic details were known to just about everyone—the name of the hero, Albert, for instance—but the sheer depth of Bell's knowledge was enough to impress even Tsubaki, Narfi, and the others. Only Lefiya refused to let herself be awed by the boy's expertise, finding it altogether quite insolent of him to think he could answer the questions so readily.

There were a fair amount of discrepancies in the stories and legends passed down among the different races, mostly as there was a tendency to put one's own race's heroes on a pedestal. A hero in the dwarven legends, for instance, was nothing but a stubborn, bigoted coward in the holy book of the elves. And in Amazonian stories, it was one of their own warriors who slayed the legendary beast, while the beastmen claimed no, it was one of their thieves. Needless to say, opinions varied greatly.

Information on the legends ran rampant with bias, and there were few experts on the subject to begin with. The "official" origin stories recognized by the gods were neither read nor acknowledged, as the races much preferred to believe in stories reflecting their own pride and dignity.

Dungeon Oratoria was merely one of these god-sanctioned legends. It was a massive epic spread across multiple volumes, some of which had been lost to the sands of time, making those who'd managed to read it in its entirety few, indeed.

"Okay, what about the story where Aria cuts herself in order to share her blood with someone…?" Tiona asked somewhat nervously.

"Hmm…" For the first time, Bell appeared to struggle. He brought his hands to his head, brows furrowed in intense thought. "I don't think I've ever read that one, no…"

"All right, how about Aria protecting an injured human? And that human going on to have descendants of their own?" Tione followed up in rapid succession.

"I-I feel like it may have been there, but I don't remember it specifically being mentioned…" Bell responded hesitantly. The eccentricity of the questions and lack of answers in his own memory seemed to be throwing him for a loop.

A sense of gloom settled over the group. They appeared to have hit a brick wall.

"Although…" The boy raised his head as though just remembering something. "I'm not sure about 'descendants,' per se, but…Albert the Great did supposedly have a child."

"*What?!*" Tiona burst out. "I've never heard anything about this!" Her eyes grew as round as saucers. "Did you read the original version? The very first one from a thousand years ago?"

"Erm, well…no, but…it was more like…something my grandpa drew."

Tiona blinked incredulously.

Even Tione and the others were taken aback.

"Did you grandfather…write picture books?" Tiona's eyes narrowed in scrutiny.

"Ha-ha…ha-ha-ha-ha…erm, well, how should I put it?" Bell's face twitched as he let out an awkward laugh.

If anything, what his grandfather told him was probably more of a dramatization of the story to appeal to children, not something they could actually rely upon. That was what the majority of the tent quickly thought to themselves, their concentration already waning.

Tione, however, remained intensely focused on the conversation.

"What happened to the kid, then? I remember at the end of Albert's story…"

"Yeah, he got involved in that battle…then just disappeared."

The interrogation on the tent floor continued as the two faced each other, the boy kneeling and Tiona sitting cross-legged.

"By the way, who were the women in his party again?" Tiona continued. "I mean, if he had a kid…"

"There was, uh…the Amazonian empress Ivelda and…the high elf queen, Celdia."

The moment the high elf's name passed from his lips, every elf in the tent was on her feet.

"—And just what the hell are you implying here?! Lady Celdia is an eternal saint! Devoid of impurities! The pride of our people, who left her own home on a quest to save the world! It's unthinkable that she would ever have a child with someone of another race!!" Alicia began.

"All our nobles are descended from Lady Celdia's younger sister Lady Rishena! Including our very own Lady Riveria!" Lefiya continued.

Bell's shoulders jumped; even Tiona and the others were startled by the outburst from the two red-faced elves.

"We already have our own bumbling stooges calling themselves 'royalty' and spreading rumors about some 'orphan' of Lady Celdia's starting their own sect or what have you…and now you're saying we should believe them?!"

"A violation of majesty!" Even Lefiya found herself overcome with rage this time. The holy book that had graced every elf village without fail and the high elf she so revered were now under direct attack.

"I'm so sorry, I'm so sorry, I'm so soooooooooooorry!!" Bell wailed tearfully as the two beautiful, seething elves closed in on him.

"Alicia! Lefiya! Calm down!" Tiona shouted as she and the others attempted to intervene.

From outside the tent, onlookers cocked their heads in curiosity at the commotion disturbing the tranquil camp.

"While this has certainly been insightful…we're not really any closer to the heart of the matter—what any of this has to do with Aiz."

It was a short while later.

Tione and the others had set Bell free, the girls once again in their circle in the middle of the tent and hunched over in thought.

Why was it that Aiz found herself a target of both the creatures and demi-spirits? As the circle hmmed and racked their brains, Lefiya couldn't help but feel a twinge of melancholy at the fact that her beloved Aiz hadn't felt it necessary to let them in on her secret.

"—You all really shouldn't be prying like this."

A sudden voice called from the tent's entrance.

The flap of cloth was pushed aside, and a new face joined them.

"L-Lady Riveria!"

"Wh-why are you here?!"

Lefiya and Tione were startled.

"As if no one would notice the giant commotion you all were making." Riveria's long jade-colored hair swayed as she let out a sigh. The noise inside the tent had reached such a fevered pitch, in fact, that Finn and the others in the main tent had sent her to check things out.

As the discerning eye of the high elf passed over each of them, Alicia and Lefiya instinctively shrank back.

Only Tsubaki seemed unfazed by the elf's appearance. "It's fine, ain't it? We were just havin' a little talk," she asserted with a shrug.

"...You know, Riveria. Don't you think this secret of Aiz's is something we should be aware of? I mean...we're all in the same familia here," Tiona said directly, her brows furrowed as she rose to her feet.

Riveria's face was pensive as she replied, her eyes never leaving Tiona's. "I won't deny the fact that we as a familia are connected by a strong bond. Having said that, I'm sure there are also plenty of you who've not revealed your entire life's story to the rest of the group."

"!"

"How would you like being forced into revealing your secrets?"

Lefiya's and Aki's eyes widened in surprise as Tiona and Tione averted their gazes with simultaneous shudders.

"...I do understand how you feel. I really do." Riveria closed her eyes.

"Right..."

"The fact that Aiz still cannot speak of it is a shortcoming on her part. And the fact that we, too, allow her to conceal it is something we take full responsibility for. I'm sure you feel we're not acting in good faith...especially as all of you witnessed the events on the fifty-ninth floor." Riveria opened her eyes, letting them travel across the group. "Though I cannot explain everything without Aiz herself present..." she said, "...I can say for certain that Aiz is, indeed, blessed with the blood of a spirit."

"You're sure you still can't tell Tiona and the others?"

They were back in the main tent. Riveria had already vacated her seat.

The glow of magic-stone lanterns flickered like candlelight in the wide tent. The flap of the tent was securely closed, and Aiz let her gaze fall as if in response to Finn's question.

"...I feel like...if I told them...it would only make me weaker." Her words were slow and deliberate. "If I were to tell them...and accept their kindness...it would change me again...and I think I won't be able to become stronger."

"You think you're being strong, but you're not..." Finn whispered, though the words were inaudible to Aiz.

Instead, it was Gareth who spoke up next, sitting next to Finn as he addressed the girl bound by her all-encompassing desire. "I'm sure there's more to it than that, lass. Go ahead. It's only Finn 'n' me here. Don't keep it bottled up inside ye so."

Aiz's gaze fell.

At long length, the words began to spill from her lips, a little at a time.

"I'm...afraid...of how they'll look at me...once they know."

It was a reason easy enough for Finn and Gareth to understand, given that they'd watched over her, protected her since she'd been nothing more than a child.

She wasn't the mystical Sword Princess who everyone made her out to be. No, the girl in front of them now—the lost, wandering little girl just trying to find her way—was the real Aiz Wallenstein. They knew this. So did Riveria.

Silence settled over the tent.

"...I think you're makin' a mountain out of a molehill," Gareth said finally.

And as the old dwarf stroked his beard with a hearty grumble, Finn couldn't help but chuckle under his breath.

"Aiz hasn't been the same since that red-haired creature Levis appeared. I'm sure it was never something she wanted to discuss, nor the connection it had to her blood."

Lefiya and the others were still in shock as they listened, their suspicions surrounding Aiz's lineage now confirmed.

Riveria's eyes turned glassy for a moment, as though she were staring at something far, far off, then she continued. "It was never Aiz's intention to reveal her past, even with this turn of events."

"..."

"Someday, however, that time will come...and until it does, I ask that you wait," she finally finished, entreating the group the same way a mother would. "I also ask that...once you do know, you treat her no differently than you have in the past."

It grew silent.

But only for a moment, because almost instantly, Tiona was walking forward, a broad smile on her face. "'Course!" she started. "I mean, we're a familia, after all. Right, Riveria?" she added with a childlike laugh. "Aiz is just, well, Aiz!"

The words were enough to bring the rest of the tent to their feet in agreement.

"Indeed. Don't you think we're past this point by now?"

"A-as if I would ever, ever avoid Miss Aiz! Not in all of eternity!!"

Tione and Lefiya assured her respectively, though the red-faced Lefiya was the only one who did so with an undaunted sense of competition. The others in the tent—Aki, Alicia, Narfi—all responded, as well, with somewhat chagrined yet affirmative nods. Tsubaki looked out across the gaggle of girls with a contented smile on her face.

Riveria's eyes softened in a smile as her lips curled upward.

"Thank you, everyone."

1/3
PURE
PASSION

Гэта казка іншага сям'і.

◆

1/3 чыстай страсці

"*What?!* Y-you want me to go on a date…I-I-I mean sightseeing with that boy in Rivira?!"

It was "morning" on the eighteenth floor.

Loki Familia's camp had grown decidedly more cramped after the arrival of Hestia and the rest of her rescue party the night prior. In the midst of the increased bustle, Aiz had just informed Lefiya of the day's plans, which had prompted the elf's somewhat intense outburst.

The group had already finished eating their breakfast.

As it was Bell's and the others' first times on the eighteenth floor, and they planned on leaving together with *Loki Familia* anyway, it seemed they were to take advantage of the time they had and do a bit of sightseeing. Aiz was accompanying him as a guide, along with Tiona and Tione, both of whom had free time to spare.

Hearing all of this now with the group of "tourists" standing in front of her, Lefiya found herself completely disoriented.

"Yeah! You wanna come, too? It'll be more fun if we go together!" Tiona suggested with a smile.

"But I…I…I couldn't possibly leave my nursing duties…!!" Lefiya replied, her voice strained.

While Aiz and the others might have been familia elites, Lefiya herself was just a mid-level member. It was her responsibility as one of the lower ranks to ensure all miscellaneous tasks around the campsite were attended to.

While it was true that after the plethora of food prepared yesterday, there wasn't as much to do today, this didn't mean she could just abandon the tasks she'd been assigned, and this morning she'd been assigned a three-hour nursing shift to help take care of the wounded.

"Stop bugging her, will you? Look, you're making her uncomfortable," Tione berated her sister.

"N-no, it's...I mean...I don't mind...!"

She wanted to go.

She wanted to go with her.

She wanted to keep an eye on the shameless, insolent boy who'd somehow gotten Aiz to lead him around the city, and she wanted to put a stop to his nefarious plans. She was also hoping to spend time with Aiz and the others, too, of course.

She opened her mouth once. Twice.

"Erm...sorry, Lefiya...?" Aiz finally piped up, an apologetic look on her face.

No doubt, the golden-haired, golden-eyed swordswoman felt guilty for leaving Lefiya and the others behind to do all the work. Lefiya herself felt no resentment at this. In fact, she would be the one feeling guilty if the familia elites were forced to participate in such menial tasks. Their fatigue couldn't be compared to that of the lower-level members, what with the horrific battle they'd waged in the Dungeon's depths, and she hoped only that they'd spend time resting and recovering.

Which was why she didn't care that they were leaving. Not at all. She didn't care...in the slightest...that they were leaving.

Her insides churned.

As she watched them walk away, smiling with Hestia and the rest of her party, Lefiya groaned inwardly.

"I'll...I'll come join you! As soon as I've finished my work!" Raising her shapely eyebrows, she darted forward to grab Aiz's hand.

"Hm...? Ah, okay." Aiz simply cocked her head to the side in confusion at the elf's sense of duty. "Don't push yourself, okay?" she added before walking over to join Bell and the others.

"Be back soooooon!" Tiona called out with a wave of her hand, and then the group was on their way to the town of Rivira, leaving Lefiya and their other companions behind.

"Rakuta! Do we need water?! The healers aren't calling, are they?! It's time to bathe everyone!"

"I-i-it's fine, Lefiya! Everything's...already taken care of. You don't need to shout like that..."

Lefiya got straight to work caring for their poison-afflicted companions, flinging herself into her duties with every ounce of will she could muster, like an elf possessed. Her companions, however, were sleeping peacefully in their tents, and the hume bunny who was her nursing partner started turning pale as she desperately tried to quiet the boisterous elf.

I have to finish as fast as I can to join up with Aiz and the others...! Or, at least, that had been her plan, but her actions so far seemed to be having the opposite effect. Her intensity was only exhausting her already exhausted companions all the more.

She could already hear Riveria scolding her in her mind as she continued her mad rush. *"What were you thinking putting your companions through even more suffering?!"*

"It seems all I've done is be scolded lately..." Lefiya moaned to herself, eyes filled with tears of anguish as she busied herself washing the bodies of the sick with the water she'd drawn from the stream.

Dipping her cloth into the helmet filled with cool, fresh water, she gently wrung out the excess moisture before placing it atop the forehead of her bedridden companion.

Even as she thought back to her own failures, however...she found that every single one of them could be attributed to that white-haired human boy. And the thought made her gleaming eyes fill with tears.

I know I shouldn't think so ill of him, but...!

She couldn't help it.

He was constantly poking his nose into Aiz's business.

It didn't matter how thickheaded he was. And Aiz's interest in the boy?

Did it come from actual affection for him or his surprising rate of growth? Lefiya didn't know for sure, but what she did know was that the power-craving Sword Princess she knew had changed and would continue to change the longer she chased after that rabbit.

And from Lefiya's perspective, the perspective of a girl who'd long adored Aiz from afar, this was not okay.

Just being near him was enough to make her see red.

Just as she'd first dubbed him her rival back during their special training sessions with Aiz.

But should I really be fighting with him over something like this...? No, but he's the one from a different familia here! He should be showing a little restraint! A little modesty...! she grumbled to herself, lips pouting and hands shaking. Every thought led her straight back to pure frustration toward that boy.

At any rate, she had work to do! Work she needed to complete if she had any hopes of joining Aiz and the others in whatever they happened to be doing with Bell and his goddess.

And so Lefiya threw herself into her duties, caring for her afflicted companions, wiping down their sweat-soaked bodies, and occasionally making the trip to the small stream for water when her supplies ran low.

"Lefiya! Shift change. We'll take over from here."

"Ah, right!"

She'd been so focused, time had seemed to pass in an instant, and already Alicia and the rest of the second shift had arrived.

As soon as she was outside the tent, Lefiya felt her heart soar, and she turned to rush off after Aiz and the others.

However, the moment she pointed herself in the direction of Rivira's lake to the west...

"Lefiya. You have a visitor."

"Hm?"

A voice called out to her, stopping her in the middle of her trek across camp.

It was Cruz Bussell, a chienthrope and one of the lower-level members who had accompanied them to the fifty-ninth floor, the same as Raul and the others. A man of few words, he simply pointed toward the camp's southern border.

"An elf girl. Seems she's here to see you," he continued. "She's from a different familia, so she's waiting just outside camp."

"Thank you," she responded in blank puzzlement before wandering over to take a look for herself.

An elven visitor...? Who in the world could it be?

Her head cocked to the side, she jogged toward the edge of camp to where, true to Cruz's words, an elf with long obsidian hair stood waiting in her pure-white battle clothes.

Lefiya's blue eyes met the visitor's red ones, and her heart jumped in surprise.

"Miss Filvis!"

Her jog changed to a run as she dashed forward, all smiles.

Filvis Challia.

A second-tier adventurer and member of *Dionysus Familia*. She was the captain of her familia, and she and Lefiya had first become acquainted during the events in the pantry on the twenty-fourth floor, and they'd had somewhat occasional contact since.

"You are all right...It's been a while." The other elf's lips formed a smile of her own. She looked relieved to see Lefiya in one piece.

Lefiya came to a stop in front of her, looking up just slightly to meet the taller elf's eyes.

"Why are you here?"

"There were rumors from someone in Rivira who'd returned to the surface to replenish their supplies. They said *Loki Familia* had returned from their expedition and had set up camp in the forest on the eighteenth floor," Filvis explained.

It would seem their return was already a hot topic up on the surface.

"I wanted to know how you were, so I requested some time off from Lord Dionysus," she continued, her crimson eyes fixed on Lefiya's face. "You've...lost weight."

"I-I have?! Was I really that large before?" Lefiya exclaimed, somewhat shocked given how she'd specifically been trying to avoid sweets during the days leading up to the expedition.

"That's not what I meant," Filvis retorted with a wry smile.

Not only had their resources been limited over the course of the expedition, but also the harsh conditions of the Dungeon itself were enough to chip away at anyone's constitution over time.

Lefiya and the others had foregone everything except the utmost of necessities—their finely honed swords, for instance, or their staves carved from the wood of the fairy forest's most sacred tree.

"You look almost…gallant. No, perhaps that's the wrong word." Filvis's eyes narrowed. Lefiya was taken aback by the implication that the expedition had changed her in some way. "Lefiya, I'm…glad you made it out alive. Seeing you again here makes me truly happy."

The words coupled with Filvis's soft gaze were enough to make Lefiya's cheeks flush pink.

Filvis, too, upon realizing what she had just said, gave a tiny start and turned her gaze away. She coughed. "Anyway, you're alive. That's what matters." She corrected herself a moment too late as a blush clearly appeared on her snow-white cheeks.

Lefiya smiled.

She was overjoyed at the emotions playing out on the other elf's countenance. To be able to talk like this again, face-to-face, filled her chest with warmth.

It was a reunion half a month in the making.

"Did, erm…anything happen while we were gone? Perhaps regarding the remnants of the Evils…?"

"Nothing. Or at least not that we could see. If anything, *Hermes Familia*'s unwarranted intervention caused the biggest stir. I wanted to get word to you as soon as possible…" Filvis couldn't keep the scowl from her face.

Lefiya responded with a curious look of her own, but Filvis simply continued with a question.

"…How did the expedition go?"

"We had no losses. While it was, indeed, extraordinarily demanding, we also…learned quite a bit," Lefiya explained, standing up straight. "We attained a great many things, both tangible and immaterial." She continued her explanation, her eyes never leaving Filvis's and her voice filled with complicated emotion. "—I wanted to thank you, Miss Filvis. I was able to use the magic you taught me to protect Miss Aiz and the others."

It had been toward the end of the battle on the fifty-ninth floor.

Lefiya had used her Summon Burst, conjuring Filvis's spell of protection, Dio Grail, to block the corrupted spirit's magic attack.

The divine, immaculate light had protected her party from almost certain death.

"If it weren't for your magic, neither I nor the others would be standing here before you today," Lefiya continued, her eyes flooding with tears of gratitude.

Filvis froze, eyes wide.

"It…I…My magic really…saved you?" she asked before slowly looking down at her right hand.

Her crimson eyes trembled, as though overcome with emotion.

Lefiya could guess what was going on in her mind—that she hadn't been able to save her own companions, her fellow familia members during the Twenty-Seventh-Floor Nightmare.

Their lives had slipped through her fingers despite her magic.

The same magic had succeeded, now, in saving those Lefiya held dear.

If Lefiya's guess was correct, what must be going through the other elf's mind?

Lefiya couldn't even begin to imagine.

All she could do was stand there, watching over Filvis in silence, as the dark-haired elf stared at her hand.

"—Lefiya."

It was then that the sound of her own name stole her attention.

It was a voice from behind her.

"L-Lady Riveria! Why are…?"

"I heard from Cruz that you had an elven visitor," Riveria explained as she approached them, jade-colored hair dancing with each step.

The two elves watched in shock as she came to a stop in front of them.

"I thought it might be you. This young elf…she is the one who taught you that spell, yes?"

"Sh-she is, yes. This is Miss Filvis Challia of *Dionysus Familia*," Lefiya responded.

At Lefiya's confirmation, Riveria nodded before examining the dark-haired elf.

Filvis, on the other hand, could only stand there in a stupor. The introduction of her queen was just too much for her.

"It was your magic that helped us turn the tide of our battle. Filvis Challia, my elven sister, I owe you the utmost gratitude. Thank you," the high elf said quietly. A smile rose to her enchanting features, which outrivaled those of all other elves.

Every muscle in Filvis's body froze.

"Lady...Riveria..." she murmured, voice cracking. But even as her body trembled, she wasn't about to allow herself to be done in by her awe. She quickly stepped away, putting distance between herself and the high-elf queen. "It brings me great honor to stand here before you today..." she said, averting her eyes. "...You'll have to excuse me." And then she turned on her heels and walked away.

"M-Miss Filvis?" Lefiya called after her in confusion, but the other elf didn't respond, simply leaving the camp in silence.

Riveria, too, could only look on incredulously as her fellow elf vacated the premises.

Something had been off about her—that much Lefiya could tell—and she quickly directed a look of confusion at Riveria.

"Don't mind me. Go after her."

"R-right! Excuse me!" Lefiya shouted behind her as she took off.

She made a beeline for Filvis.

Toward that wordless elf making her way quickly away from camp and out of the forest. Already, those flowing black locks, reminiscent of a shrine maiden's, were receding farther and farther from view.

"Miss Filvis, please wait! What's wrong?" Lefiya shouted as she raced through the trees, quickly catching up with the other elf.

Filvis didn't stop, pressing forward as she gave a stony response. "...Lady Riveria is a high elf."

"And what does that have to do with anything? There's no cause for concern!"

Riveria Ljos Alf was the strongest mage in Orario, and her name and history were well known throughout not only the city but the rest of the world, as well. There wasn't an elf in the whole world who didn't know who she was, and for a race as mindful of one another as the elves, this demanded a high degree of reverence and respect.

Lefiya could only look at Filvis in abject confusion.

"Lady Riveria treats us as equals. She's never cared for those who stand on ceremony!"

There's no need to treat her with such reverence, she tried to continue, but Filvis cut in before she could finish.

"I am unclean."

"!!"

She spat the words like a curse.

"She cannot be close to someone like me. What would I even say to her as I am now? So exposed as I am to ridicule? No, I…couldn't do it. I couldn't take it. I would end up sullying her, as well," she said, interrupting Lefiya with her own self-directed scorn.

Her normally beautiful features were contorted in bitter mortification.

"And if there was anyone in this world not to be sullied, it is her." Her heart, stained with the sins of her past, was stirring within her.

She wasn't going to stop, obstinately placing one foot in front of the other.

Lefiya watched her in silence.

The girl was both beautiful and ugly. She'd watched her companions die until she was the only one left alive, and the sin of that crime still tormented her to this day. Her elven pride only made it all the more overpowering—a stain she'd never be able to wipe away.

More than anything else, she feared sullying Riveria with that same sin.

Lefiya followed along behind her hate-filled fellow elf until, all of a sudden, she knew what she had to do.

Her eyes flashed just as they had once before, her arm extended just as it had once before, and her hand gripped the other girl's wrist just as it had once before.

"Miss Filvis!"

"!"

Filvis came to a stop.

Lefiya's shout hit her and her aura of desolation, like a slap to the face.

"Someone as dirty as you seem to think you are would not have been able to teach me that spell!"

"Gngh…"

"It was your magic. Your magic, Miss Filvis, that saved me. That saved Lady Riveria!"

Filvis was silent for a moment, her eyes wide with shock, and then she winced. She tried to shake off Lefiya's grip on her wrist, but the other girl refused to let go.

Flustered as she was, her arm had lost its strength.

"Don't misunderstand me, Lefiya! It's…!"

"I am not misunderstanding you! There's not even anything to misunderstand!"

"And where exactly is this confidence coming from, hm? There's absolutely no basis for it!"

"But there is, Miss Filvis! There is! Even Loki herself said it. You may be cold and calculating on the outside, but on the inside, you have so much heart. So much, Miss Filvis!"

"What are you even talking about?!" Filvis shot back, her anger rising. As if a joke from Loki of all people could possibly reveal any truth about her!

This girl has no evidence! No justification! she thought to herself, face red with indignation. She tried to turn away, but Lefiya wouldn't have it.

"And…and what about me? You won't allow yourself to be near Lady Riveria, but I'm okay?!" Lefiya snapped back. "What exactly am I to you, Miss Filvis?!"

"I-I never said anything like that!"

Filvis had turned her head away when she realized she wasn't getting anywhere, but at Lefiya's question, she whirled back around to face her.

Her eyes met Lefiya's, though the other elf had shrunk away a little in shame.

Filvis was quiet for a moment, face still flushed as Lefiya's azure eyes stared through her, then she dropped her gaze awkwardly.

"I-I'm going back."

"No."

"I'll do what I want!"

"I won't allow it!"

"Let go of me!"

"I will not!"

They struggled, their heavy breaths loud against the quiet of the surrounding trees. The forest leaves sheltered them from the sounds of the outside world.

At long length, Filvis shook her head as if admitting defeat.

"Are you this high-handed with the other members of your familia...?"

Lefiya stared at her blankly for a moment. Then...

It was her turn to look away awkwardly, at anything but Filvis.

"I, erm...n-not really? I would never be able to...to behave like this with Miss Aiz and the others. Just...just you."

"Just me?! Why?!" Filvis screamed, face pointed toward the sky.

The tension was starting to become uncomfortable. But even as Lefiya averted her eyes, she refused to release Filvis's wrist.

Filvis cursed under her breath...but even the curse itself came out strained, the words directed to somewhere down by her feet.

"Ever since I met you...I've felt more and more strange," she muttered, sounding altogether very lost, her face still a brilliant shade of pink.

Lefiya stilled, her own face heating up. She smiled.

Perhaps the other elf would never be able to forgive herself.

And as one who didn't even fully understand how she felt, perhaps Lefiya would never be able to do anything to assuage her pain.

But the way Filvis was changing was quite possibly one of the sweetest, most noble things she'd ever seen.

"...Why are you smiling?"

"Hee-hee-hee..."

Even under Filvis's vindictive glare, Lefiya couldn't keep the smile off her face.

Filvis closed her eyes, blocking out the brilliant grin of her companion as she turned away. A light pink touched her long ears.

The dappled light filtering in from the trees overhead painted their clasped hands.

It wasn't long after that Lefiya realized something.

She'd become so engrossed in her back-and-forth with Filvis that she'd completely forgotten about joining up with Aiz and the others in Rivira.

Before she knew it, the group had already returned to camp.

"Nooooooooooooooooo——!!"

"Hey, hey! Let's all go take a bath together!"

Tiona was the first to speak up upon their return.

"Again? How many times do we need to go before you'll settle down?"

"Aw, c'mooooooon! It's not like we're doin' anything else! And the water is just sooooooo niiiiiiiiice!"

"Noon" had arrived at the camp.

Aiz, Bell, and the others had just returned from their sightseeing jaunt to Rivira.

And Tiona's suggestion had come as soon as the girls had all gathered back together.

When the Amazonian girl declared that she liked the eighteenth floor, what she was really declaring was her love for the Under Resort's pool. Her love of bathing wasn't something restricted to the Dungeon, either. Even back in the manor, she was known for her tendency to suddenly rise to her feet and declare she was "going to the bath for a bit!" So it was no surprise that this carefree inclination carried over to the middle levels of the Dungeon, as well. The frequency of her "bath-time announcements" was enough to give the third-tiers and below especially painful headaches.

"You just want a glimpse of Lady Hestia's rack, is that it? Is all that boobage too much for you?" Tione teased, voice laced with suspicion.

"I-I do not! As if!!"

At the mention of her name, however, Hestia and the rest of her party glanced up.

"Is something wrong, Lady Hestia?" Mikoto asked, turning toward the goddess.

"Hmmm…it's just…now that they mention it, it would be really nice to get clean. What about you guys, hm? Should we join them?"

"If we can, I suppose I'd be up for it…What about you, Lady Chigusa?"

"M-me…? I…All right," the prum responded meekly as the rest of the familia offered their opinions.

The two *Takemikazuchi Familia* women in the rescue party, both of Far Eastern descent, gave reserved yet distinct nods.

"…Lord Hermes?" Asfi turned around to ask her patron deity, her snow-white cape fluttering.

"Hm? Ah, no worries. Feel free to take a break from your guard duties if you'd like," Hermes responded languidly, temporarily freeing his usual escort from her responsibilities.

"You too, Aiz!" Tiona called out, latching herself onto Aiz's back.

"Okay…"

"Go invite Leene and the others. We can take shifts," Tione said, and the bathing party expanded quite rapidly.

Soon, every one of the familia's female members was being invited.

"Are you coming, Lefiya?" Aiz asked the young elf.

"…"

"Lefiya?"

"………"

Lefiya, however, didn't respond. In fact, she didn't move a muscle and simply stood there, still as a tree, staring blankly off into space.

She had gotten so excited about meeting Filvis again that she hadn't been able to join the group for their sightseeing trip in Rivira, and it had left her in a sort of stupor. To think that she'd forget her one true goal! It was an inconceivable defeat.

To make matters worse, the reason for her lapse in memory, Filvis, had already left in a huff after Lefiya had cornered her, the tips of her ears still bright red.

As Aiz looked upon the living elf statue, she was quite perplexed.

"Snap out of it, Lefiya! Bath time! Let's go!" Tiona flung herself at the stupefied elf, the impact breaking her out of her trance.

"Huh?!" Lefiya shook her head back and forth in an attempt to ascertain the situation. "B-bath time? Ah, I'll go, I'll go! I shall join you! I won't lose to that human this time!" she asserted, still not fully recovered.

"Erm...okay?" was all Aiz could say, even more startled at Lefiya's seemingly irrelevant statement.

"Then let's go! Let's go!" Tiona cried out, still attached to Lefiya's side, and then they were off.

There were twenty of them including Hestia and her group. The lower-level members stuck out like sore thumbs, and Tsubaki was nowhere to be seen, currently off wandering about who knew where. Tiona took the lead, guiding the girls so triumphantly that even Hestia's group, who'd yet to even break a sweat since they'd entered the Dungeon, found their excitement building.

The large party made its way along.

Until, after a short while, the scene in front of them expanded to reveal a breathtaking waterfall.

"Heeeeeeeere we are!" Tiona splayed her arms out in a show of grand exaltation.

"Oooooooh!" the awed group chorused.

Clear blue water cascaded down the some ten-meder height of the waterfall. The faint spray dancing along the pool's surface was both cool and refreshing. It was surrounded on all sides by the dim glitter of crystal, the view overhead a vast, dome-like canvas of leaves and branches.

It was the same fountain pool Aiz and the others had enjoyed only two days prior.

"While I knew there were pools in this forest...I hadn't known about this one," Asfi murmured as she admired the scenery. Though she'd been to the eighteenth floor many a time, this was the first time she'd been to this pool.

"Tiona was the one who found it..." Aiz explained with a little smile. "...She discovered this hidden treasure during one of her strolls."

Despite this particular pool being a bit of a trek from the campsite, visiting it whenever they had time had become a sort of *Loki Familia* custom.

"Shall we take turns, then?" Tione suggested. "...Lady Hestia, if you and your party would like to go first..."

"No, no, you guys should feel free to go first! We're fine going second."

"Just leave guard duty to us!"

"Really? All right, then..."

When Tione looked around at her own familia, ignoring the first-timers for now, the lower-level girls gave up their places for their senior sisters. She responded with a smile as the young demi-humans chorused, "We'll keep watch, too!"

While the eighteenth floor may have been a safety point, that didn't stop monsters from other floors from making their way to this forest in search of food. It would be senseless to bathe without someone keeping watch—that rule applied no matter which floor of the Dungeon they happened to be on.

And that didn't even go into the many men lurking about the forest, as well.

"I'll go ahead and get in, then, Lefiya."

"Be my guest, Miss Aiz!"

And so Lefiya found herself once again on guard duty.

There were eight who made their way into the pool first, including Aiz, Tiona, and Tione, as well as Hestia and Asfi of the rescue party.

There was no hesitation among them, all of the girls laughing and talking as they began removing their clothes in preparation for the bath.

The new girls, led by the imperious Mikoto Yamato of the Far East—the up-and-coming *Takemikazuchi Familia* rookie known even among the other adventurers—boasted gorgeous bodies with supple arms and legs and smooth, perky curvatures that could rival the *Loki Familia* members'.

"—Hmph! I think we can all agree that I'm the winner here!" Hestia proclaimed triumphantly—at Aiz, for some reason—as she made a grand show of removing her own garments.

Even Aiz was taken aback at the twin mountains tumbling out of the goddess's restraints, but it was Tiona who suffered the biggest emotional hit, bringing an arm up to cover her own flat chest with a strangled cry of defeat.

Tione, on the other hand, didn't seem bothered in the least. "Take a look," she said.

Once the group finished relieving themselves of their clothes, they headed immediately for the pool.

"Yaaaaaahooooooo!"

"What have I told you about diving in like that, Tiona?!"

"Oh! This really is something!"

"The water is absolutely beautiful...even the streams of our home in the East weren't this clear."

"It really feels wonderful..."

"You know, you're actually quite elegant, Miss Asfi. I never noticed it before."

"Are you saying I'm not normally, Lilliluka Erde...?"

"N-no, uh...just that...you know, you're always giving one hundred percent to your work!"

Voices rose from all over the pool as the group enjoyed themselves, some of the women diving straight into the water while others simply poured it over their skin, savoring the refreshing purity.

Even Aiz and her companions, already used to this bathing experience, were drawn in by the excited antics of Hestia and the other newcomers. Tiona's splashing led to a contest among the girls, and soon their high-pitched squeals filled the air like those of water nymphs.

Wet hair clung to their necks and shoulders as rivulets of water traced the curves of their bare skin, more lustrous and refreshing than alluring.

*They're all so beautiful…well, of course Miss Aiz is, but even the others, too…*Lefiya thought to herself with a sigh as she scanned the group from her spot outside the pool. Their naked bodies seemed so stunning in the water. And from the murmurings of the other lower-level girls dotting the perimeter, she wasn't alone in her thoughts.

At least Loki isn't here. She found herself silently thanking the sky.

The lecherous goddess would, no doubt, be foaming at the mouth already at the sight of all these naked women.

And what a sight it was, if it was enough to mesmerize even the decidedly female Lefiya.

The men would be thinking the same thing…

After all, if even Lefiya was thinking it, surely the men would be.

While their job as guards was mostly to keep an eye out for monsters…they also had a duty to bestow divine judgment unto any and all degenerate Peeping Toms who might try catching a glimpse of female skin. Lefiya's staff was ready to create hellfire at a moment's notice.

That being said, Aki and the other girls were still back at camp to keep an eye on *Loki Familia*'s men. Any libidinous intentions they had were sure to be stymied then and there. Plus, the perimeter they'd made to guard the pool was impenetrable. Anyone who tried to sneak in would be spotted immediately.

A little smile rose to Lefiya's lips. She was entranced as she watched Aiz push a lock of golden hair behind her ear, but even still, she never let her guard down, eyes and ears keen as she monitored the environs.

It was simply unthinkable anyone would try to sneak past them to get a glimpse of the pool. In broad daylight? With such tight security, no one would—

"—EEEEEEEEEEEEEEEEEEEEEEEEK!!"

There was one.

All of a sudden, something came plummeting down from the sky with a high-pitched shriek.

It fell right smack in the center of the pool in which Aiz and the others were currently bathing.

"—Huh?!"

The *kersplash!* was accompanied by a giant spray of water.

The screams were quick to follow, and Hestia and the other girls scrambled back in terror.

A hoarse cry of surprise escaped Lefiya's lips, same as the other guards as the commotion rapidly built.

It was unthinkable! Some pig had actually been lurking about in the dense thicket of trees above their heads.

A dishonorable voyeur of a man—who'd just launched a full-scale attack on the maidens' bath!!

For an instant, time seemed to stand still, then Lefiya jerked forward.

Her face paled instantly. The degenerate who had come tumbling into her field of vision, who was currently stumbling and crawling toward the shoals, was none other than that white-haired boy.

"Huh? Little Argonaut? You wanna take a bath, too?"

"Amazing. Nothing fazes you, does it?"

Tiona and Tione stood chatting cheerily over the boy, not bothering to hide anything and showing no signs of embarrassment.

"Wha…? Wha-wha-wha…?!"

"H-huhhhhh…?!"

The same was not true of the two Far Eastern girls, who quickly plunged into the water, faces red as they let out simultaneous screams.

"It couldn't be…Lord Hermes?" Asfi mused in disbelief as she scrutinized the rustling dome of leaves overhead.

"What the hell are you doing, Bell…?" Hestia questioned, her breasts floating atop the water's surface.

"M-Mister Bell! How did you get here?!" the prum girl next to her squeaked.

And then—

"…Oh."

His gaze met Aiz's. The swordswoman currently was standing in the middle of the pool with her back to the cascading waterfall.

Her reaction was immediate, cheeks a brilliant red as she hurriedly used both hands to cover herself.

A single drop of water worked its way teasingly down from her long golden hair, across her pearly skin, tracing the nape of her neck before sliding down her slender waist.

Bell's face grew so hot it was as though a fever had taken hold of his body.

Lefiya's face, too, turned a deep scarlet.

He'd seen her.

He'd seen the naked body of her golden-haired, golden-eyed swordswoman.

He'd witnessed every inch of that gorgeous body, so beautiful it outrivaled even the gods', a body that belonged to her most cherished, most adored, most revered woman in the whole wide world.

—It wasn't possible.

Bell and Lefiya.

The former of whom was currently dying of embarrassment, the latter of whom was currently bubbling over with rage.

Both of them lost it at the exact same moment.

"*You—bastaaaaaaaaaaaaaaaaaaaaaaaaaaaaaaaaaaaaaaaaaaaaaaaaa aard!!*"

"*I'm—sorrrrrrrrrrrrrrrrrrrrryyyyyyyyyyyyyyyyyyyyyyyyyyyyyyyy!!*"

The screams erupted from their lungs simultaneously.

Then Lefiya was off, her feet pounding the ground and accelerating toward him at an impossible speed.

At the same time, Bell flung himself out of the pool with the ferocity of a river breaking through a dam.

The other guards were quick to follow, shaking off their stupor and galloping toward the white-haired boy from all sides.

But Bell was faster.

Lefiya shot through the air, her fingers outstretched, but they fell mere celches short of the boy's backside as the rabbit narrowly escaped the rapidly tightening circle of girls.

In the blink of an eye, he was gone.

"————————————————————————————————Gggnnhh!!"

A strangled noise of unadulterated fury squeezed out of Lefiya's lungs as she gave chase. Aiz and the others still in the pool were able to do nothing but stand there in shock.

Both hunter and hunted were equal shades of scarlet.

But try as she might, she couldn't seem to gain on him. He was too fast. The rabbitlike speed granted by his sheer terror was enough to surpass even their difference in level.

The intensity of his humiliation had triggered a *limit off.* Of all the…!

Ever so surely, the zooming boy grew smaller and smaller in her sights.

"—*Unleashed beam of light, limbs of the holy tree. You are the master archer. Loose your arrows, fairy archers. Pierce, arrow of accuracy!!*" It was the fastest she'd ever cast a spell in her entire life.

"Lefiya, no! What the hell are you thinking—?!"

"You're gonna kill him!!"

"He'll burn right up!!"

The other guards shouted as they began to catch up with her.

The magic she was currently weaving was easily at a Level 5 with the pure, unadulterated rage built up behind it, and what was worse, it was a homing spell. It would kill him instantly.

The demi-human girls tried desperately to save the Level-2 white rabbit from a swift and certain death. They clung to her waist, her shoulders, her back in an attempt to restrain her, just in time for her to watch the boy disappear completely into the trees in front of her.

"WUUUUAAAAAAAAAAAARRRRRRRRGGGHHH————!!"

The roar that ripped its way out of her lungs echoed throughout the entire forest.

"That damn brat saw Miss Aiz and the others in the bath!"

"I'm gonna kill him, I'm gonna kill him, I'm *gonna kill hiiiim*!!"

News of Bell's peeping incident spread across the camp like wildfire.

The men and women of *Loki Familia* instantly took up arms, glaring at him with bloodred rage. They had a new monster to kill. Even those still bedridden from poison rose to their feet like bloodthirsty zombies, driven by their unbridled fury.

The camp was roaring with battle cries as the adventurers readied themselves for war.

"What the hell?…Somethin' happen while I was away?" Tsubaki mused, having just returned from hunting. Even she was thrown for a loop by the murderous aura occupying the camp.

"I'd quite like to know myself…" Riveria closed her eyes, massaging her temple.

"Night" had fallen on the Dungeon.

Even as the light of the crystals faded and a curtain of darkness blanketed the campsite, its inhabitants were wide awake, fueled by their thirst for blood. The sight of all those ferocious visages in the flickering light of the magic-stone lanterns was enough to make Hestia and the other visitors gulp in fear.

"Bell's really done it this time…"

"He is a man, after all…"

Welf and Tsubaki murmured quietly among themselves once they'd gotten wind of what had happened.

"What the hell were you thinking, Hermes? Egging Bell on like that?!"

"C-calm down, Hestia. My pride as a god wouldn't allow me to lead Bell down any path aside from that of righteousness…"

Meanwhile, Hermes was currently being restrained in another corner of the camp.

Asfi had sensed right away that it was him lurking up in the trees with Bell, and she'd gone after him at once, leaving him no time to escape. Her ogre-like interrogation powers—the same that had earned her the alias Perseus—quickly drew out the unsavory scheme of her patron deity. Bell, himself, had attempted to thwart it, but it had ultimately led to the boy's participation and untimely fall into the pool itself.

"Don't imply Bell actually wanted to go along with your sick plan!" Hestia shot back, her twin pigtails flying as she delivered a sharp *smack!* to Hermes's oh-so-innocently smiling face. "I just knew something felt off about this whole thing…!" she continued, positively bristling. She hadn't been able to wrap her head around how on earth her weak-willed follower could have performed such an audacious act, but it all made sense now.

"Any last words, Hermes?"

"—To peep is to love, Hestia!"

"Oh, go rot in hell!"

"GrrrrrrruuuuuuAAAAAAAAAAAAAAAAAAARRRRRRRRRRGGGHHH!!"

Asfi's punishment fell swift and sure. The honor of her familia was at stake.

Hestia and the rest of *Loki Familia* could only shudder in horror as the woman inflicted a terrifying beating, her face red with shame and anger.

"So it was nothing but gods stirring up trouble after all."

"Really? Then Little Argonaut wasn't actually coming to hang out with us?"

"So…where did he go?" Aiz mused, turning her gaze away from Tione, Tiona, and the currently tortured Hermes to survey the campsite.

Bell had yet to return from his run out of the forest, his location currently unknown.

No one at the camp had seen him since he'd left.

As late as it was now, Aiz couldn't help but worry…though that thought was forgotten for a moment when a figure suddenly appeared from the direction of the seventeenth-floor passageway.

"Yeesh! The hell is all this racket?!"

"Hm? Oh! Bete!"

The werewolf scowled as he took in the sight of his strangely murderous familia members and the suffering screams of one unlucky god. A backpack stuffed full of vials hung from his right shoulder.

He'd just returned from the surface with all the antivenin he could find.

"Geez, you're late! We've been wastin' away here!"

"I'd like to see you make the trip, huh, you damn ingrate!"

"Captaaaaaaaaain! Bete's back!"

"Oh, uh…welcome back…"

Almost instantly, the pestilential atmosphere of the camp turned to flurried confusion as everyone rushed to heal the afflicted.

Vials of antivenin passed from hand to hand before being rushed to tents to be administered to their bedridden companions. The moment the rather vile-smelling purplish liquid touched their tongues, their panting gasps and raspy breaths stilled, eliciting cries of joy from the too few overworked healers. Everyone in the camp began clasping their hands in relief at the improved condition of their peers.

"Thank god! Everyone's gonna be all right!…Guess ol' Grumpy Wolf really can pull through every now and then."

"Heh. Well, at any rate, we can rest easy for now."

Tiona and Tione exchanged smiles as they watched their female companions grin in their sleep in blessed relief from the pain. Even Hestia and the rest of her party lent a hand to hasten the healing efforts.

"Good work from you, Bete. You really saved us."

"Yer clothes are an unsightly mess. Ye gods, lad! Did ye not stop for even a moment's rest?"

Riveria and Gareth both chuckled as they turned their attention toward the werewolf, who simply growled in return. "Aw, can it, you old fogies. Finn, I'm hittin' the sack!"

Bete didn't even throw them a second glance as he stormed into one of the tents.

"No worries. Get some rest…and thank you, Bete." Finn folded his arms, offering a mixture of sympathy and appreciation as he watched Bete collapse onto one of the beds.

The stifling cloud of gloom that had been permeating the entirety of *Loki Familia*'s camp since they'd arrived finally began to dissipate.

"...Hey, um, Lefiya?"

"..."

Despite the sudden excitement overtaking the campsite, Lefiya didn't seem to have noticed, simply tending to the sick in silence by herself in one of the tents.

Aiz called out to her as she passed by with another handful of antivenin but received no response. The group of hume-bunny girls Lefiya was currently administering the medication to shuddered.

Why does this feel...familiar...? Aiz thought to herself, cold sweat dribbling down her temple as she felt the dark miasma surrounding the elven maiden.

There was something foreboding about this. Like the calm before the storm.

...He still hasn't come back.

They'd already finished administering the rest of the antivenin, and a sense of peace had befallen the campsite.

Aiz let her gaze travel toward the darkened ceiling, which was hidden behind a shroud of leaves and branches.

This time belonged to the monsters of the forest. The darker it became, the harder it was to see and the greater the danger. A danger was all the more real for a lone upper-class adventurer who'd only just reached Level 2. Perhaps he was already lost, roaming the forest aimlessly in search of a way out.

Aiz knew sending out a search party now was both reckless and pointless. The forest was too vast and the boy far too small...and yet. As suppertime approached, she couldn't help but worry that she should be out there searching for him.

"Thank you so much, Miss Lyu!"

"No worries. I'll take my leave now."

—It was then that it happened.

The moment Aiz turned in the direction of the waterfall pool, Bell and another adventurer appeared from among the trees.

It was someone Aiz was sure she'd seen before...someone from the rescue party, wearing a mask.

At dinner the night before, yes. Aiz was sure she'd seen them talking to Bell. They'd come together with Hestia and the others, an enigma enshrouded in that hood and long cape they never seemed to remove. Even now, their face was concealed. The slim frame adorned in shorts and long boots beneath lightweight battle clothes, however, appeared decidedly female.

Identity aside, it would seem as if this girl had located the wandering Bell and brought him home.

After exchanging what appeared to be a few words with the boy, she returned silently to the forest.

Aiz let out a sigh of relief.

No sooner had the breath passed her lips, however, than the bedraggled Bell started his way toward her with a sigh of his own, gaze rising to meet hers…and their eyes locked.

"Ah."

"Oh."

They verbalized in unison.

Twin blushes rose to their faces, almost as though they were looking in a mirror.

The scene from only a few hours earlier replayed in both their minds. The thought of him seeing her naked was enough to make Aiz's cheeks radiate heat; meanwhile, the thought of seeing Aiz naked was enough to make Bell's face glow red up to his ears.

"…I, uh…erm…"

She squirmed, rubbing her hands together as her eyes dropped to her feet.

This loss of composure wasn't like her. She was so flustered, she couldn't even look Bell in the face. She'd never felt like this before. Not only her cheeks but her whole body burned, every celch of her skin turning a fierce, fiery scarlet.

The boy was the same.

Even more rattled than Aiz, he was sweating enough to form a salty lake beneath his feet, until suddenly—he threw himself forward onto the ground, lying prostrate.

"I'm...I'm *so sorrrrrrrrrrrrryyyyyyyyyyyyyyyyyyyyyy*!!" he screamed. It was a shameless apology from every ounce of his being.

Aiz was stunned into silence. Quickly she attempted to put a stop to the full-bodied apology. The boy's head was already bleeding from having hit the ground a little too hard.

"I'm sorry, I'm sorry, I'm sorry, I'm sorry..." he continued somewhat deliriously as Aiz pulled him up and onto his feet with a wobble. Red still stained his cheeks, and he lowered his head so that his white bangs hid his eyes.

The sight of his continued shame was enough to bring the flush back to her own cheeks.

"It's...it's fine...really...okay?" she assured him, voice sisterly.

"O-okay..." Bell croaked, his head drooping.

And so they stood there, blushing violently, facing each other but unable to even glance up.

Time passed slowly after that.

Bell made his rounds, apologizing to each and every one of the girls who'd been present in the bathing pool. One by one. With the utmost civility. And fervently.

He spent so long on his knees, it was a surprise he didn't dig himself a hole, and at the sight of him throwing himself on the ground again and again in Far Eastern prostration, none of the girls could stay mad at him for long. When they additionally took into account the extenuating circumstances involving a certain god who'd instigated the entire affair, there was no way they could punish him beyond a harshly worded warning.

Tiona and the others weren't bothered in the least by what had happened, and they simply brushed it off with a laugh. Asfi, on the other hand, actually turned Bell's apology around, apologizing to him instead. His patron deity, Hestia, toed the border between lunacy and acumen as she gave him one of her thorough sermons, while Hermes, worn to the bone and wheezing softly, simply frightened Bell away with a hoarse hiss.

While the coed "Sword Princess Protection Unit" still had one last riot left in them, Aiz managed to quell it without incident. Even Finn and the other familia leaders could only chuckle in amusement as Bell came to them in heartfelt apology for the trouble he'd caused.

"Hah..." Bell let out what was easily his hundredth sigh as his tour of apologies finally came to an end.

His features were an amalgam of humiliation, guilt, and fatigue. He'd traversed almost the entirety of the campsite, dashing here and there with his portable magic-stone lantern, while the rest of the group readied themselves for dinner. He had nothing equipped save a weapon for his own protection.

Still battling the sense of immorality plaguing his mind, he'd finally nabbed a chance to catch his breath, when—

"_____"

—the most ominous of presences appeared behind him.

Heart clenching like a vise, he gave a sudden gasp, a wheezy, high-pitched flutelike sound escaping his lips.

He turned around with an almost audible creak, sweat pouring from him, to find his forest fairy standing before him with both hands clenched murderously around her staff.

A pernicious cloud of inky black miasma rested on her shoulders, her face pointed downward in foreboding silence.

Bell couldn't move.

He'd looked death in the eyes twice already. Once when he'd taken on that minotaur, and again when Goliath had chased him on the seventeenth floor. But neither of those two fiends even came close to eliciting the deep-rooted, carnal fear running through him right now.

His rubellite eyes could almost see a terrifying dragon of magic rearing its head from behind the girl's back.

Her eyes rose.

"Unforgivable...unforgivable...unforgivable..."

Her normally azure eyes glowed with a surreal, ominous intensity.

Again and again, she continued her mantra, almost like a broken doll, looking very much like some kind of demonic entity.

He'd dirtied her. He'd sullied the immaculate body of her beloved, and the flames of antipathy were already gathering around her like a firestorm.

The staff gripped tightly in her hands let out a shrill, creaking groan.

Time stood still.

Then she seemed to sink—before jerking forward, kicking off the ground with every ounce of mind and spirit she had, and launching toward him at the speed of sound.

"Don't yooooooooooou *mooooooooooooooooooooooooooooooove*!!"

"AIIIIEEEEEEEEEEEEEEEEEEEEEEEEEEEEEEEEEEEEEEEEEEE!!"

Their grand game had begun anew.

Once more they were in heated chase, the white rabbit wailing in fear as his bloodthirsty fairy assailant ran him down.

The former boasted the leveled-up move speed of a Level 2, but the latter currently possessed the transcendent move speed of a mage driven mad by pure, unadulterated rage.

Her speed was winning, and in the blink of an eye, both pursuer and pursued were free of the camp, disappearing into the forest beyond.

"Hm? Where's Lefiya?"

"Can't find her anywhere!"

Tione and Tiona mused from the center of the campsite as they scanned the perimeter in search of the junior elf.

"…?" Aiz, too, let her eyes wander the camp. Dinner was about to begin, and Lefiya was nowhere to be seen.

Now that she was thinking about it, the boy was missing, too…

Cocking her head to the side, she couldn't help but wonder where the two had gotten off to.

The forest on the eighteenth floor was enormously vast.

The swath of skyscraping trees spanned the floor from east to west, making up a full fifth of the Under Resort's total area, and its greenery ran flush with both the sweeping grasslands at the floor's center and the enclosing walls on its every side. While a variety of fruits and vegetables grew within its verdure, foodstuffs weren't its only boon—blue crystals, too, sprang forth from its soil, from giant, swordlike formations to the smallest of tiny stones.

Perhaps its most unique trait, however, was its ability to transform into a forest of pure magic as soon as night fell upon the Dungeon.

Supplied with the whimsical light they'd built up during the "daylight" hours, the crystals glowed softly with a kind of subtle elegance, bathing the forest in a hue of blue and giving birth to an eerie, bewitching ambience. While there were, of course, the monsters to worry about, armed with their superior night vision, there were also a surprising number of trip-ups scattered throughout the forest floor, liable to lead to a world of pain for anyone lacking caution. To make matters worse, the number of upper-class adventurers who'd entered the woods and never returned was frighteningly significant, and the fact that their remains had never been found was enough to suggest that some kind of ferocious monster was lurking deep within the trees...at least, that was the story floating around Rivira.

At any rate, the forest at night was very much a dangerous place. Even those acquainted with its byways and thruways could easily lose their bearings at a moment's notice.

The reason for all this buildup was, of course, to provide transition, because, as one might expect in such a forest—

"...W-we're lost again."

"Y-you say that like it's my fault!"

—Bell and Lefiya were completely and hopelessly lost.

Their game of cat and mouse had ended right smack in the middle of the dark woods, neither one of them realizing just how far they'd come until they had no idea where they were.

Bell's head hung particularly low, as this was the second time today he'd found himself lost among these trees.

Lefiya, however, just continued her red-faced tirade, taking umbrage at everything coming from Bell's mouth.

The two novice adventurers could only pant heavily, wiping the continuous sweat from their brows as they stood beneath the lofty branches.

Lefiya had finally caught up to Bell only a few minutes prior. Just when she'd been about to strike down the frightened rabbit with her staff, she'd broken free of her trance long enough to realize nothing around her looked familiar.

The silence was deafening. The road back was unclear. And the deep, dark, spine-tingling forest all around them quickly brought reality down on them hard as they stood there in their cold sweats, silently wondering what it was they should do.

Running about recklessly would get them nowhere fast, which meant staying put was their best option for now.

"R-really, it's your fault, you know? You shouldn't have run away! And especially not this deep within the forest!"

"A-and end up dead…?! No, thank you!"

"Just what do you take me for?! I would never kill you! I only wanted to…beat you within an inch of your life, that's all!"

"Oh, because that's so much better!"

Almost as soon as they were able to breathe normally again, the squabbling started.

Bell's portable magic-stone lantern wobbled back and forth in time with his words.

"Well, you're the one who had to go and force Miss Aiz to give you special training! The impudence! You do realize you're of different familias, yes? And not even ones with amiable relations! You don't find that the least bit strange?!"

"Uhhh…"

"Miss Aiz is a first-tier adventurer! The Sword Princess! The ever-so-powerful, ever-so-beautiful, ever-so-lovely Sword Princess! She is not someone from whom lower-class nobodies can receive training! Do you not have even the slightest shred of common sense within that head of yours?!"

Before she knew it, Lefiya was rattling off everything she'd been keeping bottled up for so long. Face flushed, she closed in on the boy, leaving him cowering in fear and lost for a counterargument.

"Not only did you have the gall to monopolize Miss Aiz for a whole day—a whole day!—you then proceeded to come down here and have her waiting on you hand and foot…! I'm…I'm so *jealous*! No, I'm *appalled*!!"

"Guhhhh…?!"

She couldn't stop it now. Her insides were bubbling like a witch's cauldron, hotter and higher and more and more furious as everything came tumbling out. It was one thing after the other after another as she laid bare his every sin, from his time spent training with Aiz atop the wall before the expedition all the way until today, with her own personal grudge rearing its head from time to time.

Bell could do nothing but bend farther and farther backward beneath the onslaught.

"And then…as if that weren't enough! You…you *saw her naked body…*!!"

"I-I-I-I-I-I'm sorryyyyyyyy!!"

"You did, didn't you?!

"Huh?!"

"You saw it, didn't you?!"

"Saw what?!"

"Do you really want to make me say it?!"

"I'm so sorry, I'm so sorry, I'm so *sorrrrryyyyyyyyyyyyy*!!"

Lefiya felt tears sting the corners of her eyes at the boy's implied confession.

"Don't you feel shame as a human being? You're the worst! The absolute worst! The most vile, degenerate human being in all of existence!!" she screamed, eyes clenched shut.

It was a brilliant, scathing finishing blow, and Bell's body curled in on itself with an audible "Gnnghh!"

He took a few teetering steps backward…then let his head fall with a dramatic, soundless slump.

The girl's mighty tempest had finally passed.

"Haah…haah…" Only her ragged breathing could be heard within the dim quietude of the forest, the exertion forcing her shoulders up and down with each breath.

Still, the boy said nothing. He had no rebuttal. No excuse. His white hair hung down over his eyes like the ears of a dejected rabbit.

As the magic-stone lantern in his hand continued to exude its light, Lefiya turned her eyes away.

This was the first time since she'd met him that she'd been able to speak her mind.

She'd let everything out, all of it, and as she stood there in awkward silence now, she couldn't help but think that she'd gone too far.

Just as she began to feel truly guilty at her one-sided verbal bludgeoning of the boy…*Gurgle.*

Bell's stomach rumbled.

"…"

"…"

Though his face was still pointed downward, the tips of his ears turned visibly red.

Timidly and ever so slowly, he began to raise his head. The moment his gaze met Lefiya's, however, it snapped back down.

"That was, uh…well…Don't, uh…"

"…Are you…hungry?"

"I, erm…no? I-I mean, well…y-yes…" he squeaked, his voice growing smaller and smaller.

They'd begun their wild chase right before dinnertime. It was likely he hadn't eaten any lunch, either, running around all day as he had within the forest.

Lefiya sighed.

Their war would have to wait.

A quick survey of their surroundings yielded nothing in terms of readily available fruit. Her thoughts went, instead, to her person, and she scrounged around in her battle clothes…only to discover something located neatly in her breast pocket.

The crystal drops Aiz had given her two days prior.

Hnngh…

Her eyebrows furrowed as she eyed the two tiny teardrop shapes in the palm of her hand.

They'd been her badge of honor, so to speak, for saving her beloved, and as they sat there, glittering and sparkling in their bluish-white auras...she let out a sigh.

Taking one of the droplets between her fingers, she handed it to Bell.

"Here."

"Huh...?"

"You are hungry, are you not? While it may not be incredibly filling... it should help ease the cravings," she explained, looking everywhere but at him.

Bell seemed stunned.

Finally, though looking somewhat lost and altogether apologetic... he took the offered crystal drop.

"But...but this..."

"Just take it! It's fine!"

"O-okay!"

Even Bell could feel the shame in Lefiya's words.

Lefiya, at the same time, did her best to mask the flush rising to her cheeks by raising her voice.

"Though before you eat it, know that the value of this crystal drop is unprecedented, and you must fully savor its exquisite flavor! It could easily go for thirty thousand valis on the surface!"

"Th-thirty thousand valis for this tiny thing...?!" Bell gave a shocked shudder. It was even more expensive than the equipment on his back.

"Well, that's for an entire bottle of them...but still!" Lefiya added, a droplet of sweat working its way down her temple. She watched in awkward apprehension as he brought the tiny drop nervously to his lips, and then she followed suit.

Once the deed had been done, they took a seat somewhat unconsciously at the base of a nearby tree to get some rest.

The forest was as dark as ever around them.

The Dungeon's ceiling was all but invisible beyond the mesh-like canopy of branches and leaves above their heads. It was cold, too, no doubt a result of the faux night that had settled over the entire floor. There in the faint blue glow of the crystals adorning the tree trunk's base, the two sat side by side, Bell's magic-stone lantern placed between them and illuminating their profiles.

They said nothing, their backs to the tree as they stared into the darkness around them.

It was oppressing—this aura of awkward discomfort hanging over the two as they rolled the hard candy around in their mouths.

The strange feeling of distance between them said much about the relationship they'd formed.

"—*Ooooaaaaaahhhhh.*"

"—!"

A roar cut its way through the quiet.

The pair's shoulders twitched.

As if on cue, they looked to each other in horror.

Just the two of us, this deep in the forest…! This is no time for us to let our guards down! Lefiya thought to herself, admittedly too late.

It was dangerous in this forest at night. It was most assuredly not a place they could pleasantly pass the time until morning, at least not with just the two of them.

The last of the crystal drop dissolving in her mouth, Lefiya rose to her feet.

"We…we need to return to camp…somehow. It's too dangerous for us to remain here."

"R-right…" Bell nodded as he hurriedly followed her lead.

Lefiya quickly glanced in his direction before once again surveying their surroundings.

To the left, to the right, behind, in front, and even overhead, the trees grew thick. She couldn't make out even the slightest glimmer of light from the magic-stone lanterns undoubtedly shining brightly in Rivira or *Loki Familia*'s camp.

If I were to use my magic, Miss Aiz and the others would surely notice…wouldn't they?

Yes, a brilliant flash of light, like a firework straight overhead—the ever reliable first-tiers would definitely see it, and so long as they stayed where they were, help would be there shortly.

And yet…what kind of impression would that make?

Running off completely of her own volition, then summoning her companions to come rescue her? The shame! Lefiya had at least some self-respect.

As reluctant as she was to admit it, the fault here was entirely her own.

She had to get them out of this and safely back to camp herself.

*I simply need to pull myself together…*she thought to herself, sneaking a glance at the boy next to her, who was currently using his magic-stone lantern to scan the perimeter.

He was a Level 2, a third-tier adventurer.

She was one level higher at Level 3, a highly ranked mage and a second-tier adventurer.

When it came to both Status and experience, she had the upper hand.

"Can I perhaps…ask you something? Just how old are you?"

"Huh? I'm, uh…fourteen."

As expected, he was younger than her, as well. That would make her his senior.

Which made it all the more essential that she come up with something to get them out of this mess—a thought that made her focus sharpen.

"Don't go to pieces now, all right?! Just follow my lead and don't do anything stupid!" Lefiya was remarkably leader-like as she raised her index finger in strict instruction, her other hand still tightly gripping her staff.

"R-roger!!" Bell replied between fervent nods of his head.

Lefiya was, after all, a member of *Loki Familia*.

She couldn't allow herself to appear feckless or cowardly in front of someone from a different familia.

Pushing down the insecure little girl who so often reared her head in front of Aiz and the others, she assumed a bearing worthy of the reputation and prestige of the largest familia in all of Orario.

She wouldn't reveal the fear and anxiety fluttering in her heart. As determined fortitude flowed through her veins, she led Bell away from the tree and into the night.

Just stay calm, keep your wits about you, never let your guard down...

She took the magic-stone lantern from Bell, using it to illuminate the forest in front of her as she walked. Bell himself, she ordered to keep watch behind them.

For so long she'd been protected by, saved by Aiz and the others.

Now it was her turn. She could handle this. She had a duty.

Even if it was nothing more than a charade, Lefiya's countenance was one of a true second-tier adventurer. There was no doubt that she'd grown beyond the small, scared child always hiding behind Aiz and the others.

This was a role she'd never had a chance to fulfill, what with the entire legion of distinguished elites among *Loki Familia*'s ranks. The scared, anxious lower-level adventurer glancing to and fro behind her was her responsibility as she led him single-handedly through the forest.

She used blue crystals to denote their path, breaking off tiny pieces and scattering the glittering shards behind them as they walked. She marked their passage on the trees with a large *X*, being sure to carve it deep enough that the self-restorative wood wouldn't immediately fill the gouge back up.

And there were other times, too, that she caught wind of monsters nearby, and she and Bell would quickly snuff out the light before hiding themselves in the brush. They let monster after monster pass by them, not wanting to throw themselves into battle unless absolutely necessary.

"Erm...Miss Viridis?" the timid voice called from behind her.

"...It's Lefiya."

"Huh?"

"You may simply call me Lefiya. I'm not partial to non-elves using my tribe's name. But back to the matter at hand, do you need something?" she responded curtly, eyes trained straight forward.

"The members of *Loki Familia*...they can really do anything, can't they?" Bell asked, undaunted, as he followed behind her unfaltering forward march.

"...? What do you mean?"

"Erm, it's just...you're a mage, right, Miss Lefiya? And yet you're still so...so...I don't know, driven. Like, even right now, just charging through the forest like some kind of explorer...It's impressive. Makes me think that *Loki Familia* can do just about anything."

"D-d-driven...?!" Lefiya's cheeks flushed without warning at the boy's unadulterated praise. "F-flattery won't do you any good, you know?! We should keep all conversation to a minimum!" Lefiya whirled around in anger.

"I-I'm sorry!!" Bell immediately shrank backward.

"Really now!" she huffed, eyebrows bristling. She did not appreciate this surprise attack on her mental state.

Turning away from the boy and his look of apology, she took off at a brisk walk.

"...Miss Lefiya?"

"What is it now?" Her voice had an edge to it.

But the boy's reply was soft. "I guess...if you weren't able to do anything, you wouldn't be any help to Mister Finn and...Miss Aiz and the others...right?"

The second the words left his mouth...

Lefiya's feet came to an abrupt stop.

But only momentarily. She forced her legs to restart, attempting a slow, careful response as she pushed forward.

"This is true. If you weren't, then...then you would never be able to catch up to them."

Silence settled over the pair.

The gentle rustling of the grasses beneath their feet provided the only accompaniment to their footsteps.

For the first time, they'd reached a sort of mutual understanding. Without even realizing it, both of them existed on the same plane, their hearts beating for the same cause.

And so they continued like that for a short while.

Until what appeared in front of them was a tree so tall they had to strain their necks just to see it in its entirety.

Lefiya took a moment to survey their surroundings before beginning her investigation of the tree.

Even among the many large trees of the forest, this tree in particular was monstrously wide and skyscrapingly tall.

Perhaps this tree... Yes...

Lefiya hadn't just been arbitrarily wandering through the forest.

She'd been searching for a tree just like this one, tall and towering over the rest, from which she'd be able to ascertain their location.

Using the giant tree at the forest's center, a tree visible even from the passageway leading to the next floor, one could quickly position themselves within the vast forest, making it easier to locate a way out.

"I'm going to climb this tree and scout the perimeter. You stay here."

"Ah...okay. Roger that."

Lefiya prepped herself with a mental hurrah, then positioned herself next to the tree, fully prepared to climb the mighty giant...until she took another glance at Bell.

She instantly scowled, holding down the hem of her skirt as a flush rose to her face.

"You are not to look upward, do you understand me?!"

"Huh? I, uh..."

"Should you even think about it, you'll wish you'd never been born! Am I clear?!" Her voice rose to a threatening hiss.

"C-c-crystal!!" Bell asserted without hesitation.

Still battling the red tinge on her cheeks, Lefiya leaped from the ground with an almost audible bound, flying up into the tree and making her way toward its crown, leaving the boy behind to stand watch.

Again and again she jumped, positioning her feet on the tree's many branches.

Bell, still down on the ground with his magic-stone lantern, gave the elf a good, long period of time before he hesitantly raised his eyes skyward. Thankfully, Lefiya had already disappeared from view.

"She really can do anything..." he murmured in awe at the second-tier adventurer's hands-free ability to scale the tree using nothing but jumps.

Meanwhile, Lefiya, oblivious to the goings-on down below, leaped her way onto a particularly large branch not far from the top of the tree.

From here, it was just as she'd predicted—above the dome of green leaves, she could look out across the entirety of the floor.

She turned her gaze to the left, locating the mighty tree at the forest's center. Between her and the tree towered a giant crystal, emitting its faint blue light. It would seem they were in the eastern part of the floor—close to the easternmost tip, even.

She studied the view carefully, memorizing the lay of the land—

—when suddenly...

"Huh—?"

...her eyes dropped to the forest below.

Hastily, she hid herself within the branches' shadows.

Using the enhanced vision made possible by her Status, she trained her azure eyes on the forest floor, where she caught sight of a group of dubious figures enshrouded in long, concealing robes.

Their inky black garments melted into the surrounding shadow, completely masking their faces and identities. And, as if their robes weren't enough, each one also donned a dark hood and forehead protector, ensconcing them all the more.

Their attire was a dead giveaway—identical to the dark robes of the crew they'd battled down in the twenty-fourth-floor pantry. There was no doubt about it. These were surely associates of the Evils' Remnants.

Lefiya sucked in her breath in disbelief.

There were two of them on their way somewhere. Their destination couldn't be far.

She made a note to herself of the direction in which they were heading, then quickly bounded back down the tree.

Carving her way through the latticework of leaves, she gave one final leap before landing with a *thud* in front of the expectant boy.

Bell's eyes dilated in surprise at her sudden appearance.

"Put out the light!" she quickly hissed.

"Huh?"

"The light! Put it out!"

"R-right!"

In a flurry, he did as he was told.

Their one source of light gone, the world turned black around them. Now, at least, they wouldn't be seen by the hooded duo.

Leaving Bell to his confusion, Lefiya attempted to make sense of the situation, her mind racing.

Those two must be associates of the Evils...but what are they doing here? On this floor?

Could they be plotting something on the eighteenth floor? Were they going to do what they'd done on the twenty-fourth floor by setting loose those giant flowers and turning the pantry into a plant?

What should she do?

Return to the campsite and inform Finn and the others?

But what if they were unable to find them again? It was already a miracle as it was that she'd caught sight of them in this vast forest.

And if she tailed them, she just might be able to get more information on the series of events that had been besieging them since the Monsterphilia...

What do I do...?

Again and again, she weighed her options.

All the while, Bell continued to watch her in silence as a grim determination colored her features, and her brows furrowed.

As the seconds ticked away urgently in her mind, she finally realized what she had to do.

I need to follow them...

This was a once-in-a-lifetime opportunity if ever she'd seen one.

To be able to put a stop to their no doubt dastardly plans before the situation got out of control?

And besides, she was simply going to trail them a while—determine what it was they were doing, where they were going. That was all she needed. A simple mission, overall.

Once finished, she'd report back to Finn and the others with anything useful.

These encouraging thoughts pushing her forward, she made up her mind.

The only problem now is...

Lefiya raised her gaze.

Her eyes landed squarely on Bell, still sitting beside her in acute bewilderment.

She certainly couldn't leave him here all by himself.

Even if she told him exactly how to get back to camp (which she'd ascertained from her earlier treetop ascent), and even if he was able to follow that path all the way there, he'd have a hell of a time at his measly Level 2. And to make matters worse, he had no armor equipped—only his salamander-wool linens—and nothing but a single onyx knife for protection.

Telling him to simply sit tight and wait for her return was also out of the question.

As she sat there staring at him, and as he sat there doe-eyed and mystified, she quickly realized she had no choice.

"I...apologize, but...could you perhaps come with me for a moment?" she said before rising to her feet and vacating the premises.

Then, following the path she'd memorized from her bird's-eye view, she hurried in the direction the two Evils associates had been heading. She moved quickly, maneuvering past tree after tree, all the while attempting to mask her footsteps and stifle her pounding heart and labored breaths. Bell followed behind her in equally fervent pursuit. Though she'd quickly explained the situation, he was still far from completely understanding.

The trees and brush ran thick, making it hard for Lefiya to see where she was going, but her vigorous efforts paid off in the end, and before long, her destination came into view.

She slammed to a halt, gesturing for Bell to stop, too, then hid herself in the shadows.

I found them...!

Holding her breath, she curled her fingers tightly around the length of her staff.

They were right there, not more than fifty meders away—the two figures she'd seen from high up in the trees.

She took a moment to check that they were alone. Then, still keeping her eyes keen for signs of company, she began to follow them.

Bell stiffened next to her, not having had much choice in joining this game of cat and mouse.

"Wh-who are those people?"

"...An enemy organization. To put it simply."

"An enemy of *Loki Familia*...?" he whispered, attempting to hide himself in the dense, low-hanging foliage. Clearly, the idea of the strongest familia in Orario having any enemies, let alone the two robed figures in front of them, came as startling news.

"Look, don't ask so many questions!" she hissed back, anger evident despite her hushed tone.

"S-sorry, I won't!" Bell immediately squeaked.

Lefiya continued her careful, focused pursuit.

The two figures were also monitoring their surroundings, making steady progress despite their lack of light. And Lefiya stuck to them like glue, keeping just enough distance to ensure they wouldn't be spotted but not so much as to lose them among the dark trees. It continued like this for a short while until they finally arrived at a certain deep corner of the forest.

They were close to the Dungeon wall.

She could tell, peeking between the branches, that they'd reached the end of the line, meaning they were at the very farthest edge of the eighteenth floor's eastern side.

The forest had grown considerably sparser. Everything merged into one main path, trees and shrubberies all but gone, and even the branches and leaves overhead had thinned, leaving no room for voyeurs or assailants to hide themselves.

Scattered here and there about the open field were blue crystal pillars, all at least two meders in size. It almost looked like the ruins of a stone circle left over from the Ancient Times. The "Crystal Grove," perhaps?

As Lefiya watched, the hooded figures cut through the middle of the grove, directly for the Dungeon wall.

"There's no going back now..." Lefiya muttered to herself in encouragement. She knew they must be near her targets' goal.

Despite the butterflies dancing in her stomach, she eyed Bell meaningfully to signal their continued pursuit. Bell, despite his misgivings, nodded in response.

Leaping free of their cover, they dashed straight forward through the Crystal Grove.

They skirted from one crystal to the next, noiselessly darting in and out between the pillars.

The whole time, she kept her eyes fixated squarely on the two figures in front of her.

It was almost as if they were being led, weaving as they were, back and forth, back and forth, when suddenly—

Crack!

The ground opened up of its own accord in front of them.

"_____"

It happened the moment her foot touched down in a round clearing devoid of pillars. The mighty crack echoed around her as the earth plunged downward, creating a giant hole. Almost as though it had been *waiting* for her arrival.

"Huh...?!"

All of a sudden, she was floating. The floor disappeared beneath her. And her breath quickly got itself caught in her throat.

For a brief moment, she could feel the boy's dumbfounded presence behind her.

It took a split second for gravity to take hold.

"—Uuuaaaaaaaaaaaahhhhhhhhhhhhhhhh!!"

And then they plummeted, their screams of terror layering atop one another.

Grass, dirt, and leaves plunged with them. Lefiya's gaze rose skyward as she fell just in time to see the "lid" of the hole close up behind them with another rumble.

Cut off from the forest landscape and night Dungeon air above them, the ground rose up to meet them.

"—Unnnngh!!"

Somehow or other, both of them managed to land on their feet, the impact sending up a giant splash of *something* all around them.

The entire bottom of the hole was steeped in a light-purplish liquid.

Now that there were two additional bodies in it, the stagnant pool quickly rose from shin height to waist height with an unsettling *sqwoosh*.

""Ack!!""

It was hot. Like boiling oil. Their battle clothes sizzled against their skin.

No, not sizzled. *Melted.*

Their faces paled as they looked in horror at the bubbling, smoking liquid all around them.

"This is..." Bell's voice trembled.

"...Acid?!" Lefiya finished his thought with a scream that echoed off the walls of the hole.

While the acid wasn't strong enough to disintegrate flesh and bone instantly, the tangible feeling of the substance eating away at their skin was enough to invoke a very real sense of panic in the two adventurers. The magic-stone lantern, having fallen from Bell's hand, was now ever so slowly sinking into the liquid with a bubbling hiss, still shining its light even as the acid broke it down piece by piece.

They frantically scanned their surroundings, faces tight.

They were at the bottom of a long, deep hole.

It boasted a diameter of some seven meders and a height of at least ten.

As for the walls of the hole, they were reddish in hue and had a repulsive fleshlike texture with no sign of anything they could use as footholds or handholds.

In fact, it almost felt as if they were inside a living being, like the stomach of some treacherous beast. No matter what it was, however, the cylindrical structure they currently occupied was clearly a pitfall.

The walls of flesh gave off a faint light, coloring everything in a dim red phosphorescence, and the air felt humid and hot and carried a strange odor, quickly drawing sweat from their pores.

"Ugh…b-bones?!" Bell yelped as he let his eyes scan the perimeter.

Lefiya spun around to see for herself, only to bring her hand to her mouth in disgust.

A decomposed carcass lay sunken in the acid next to them, no doubt the remains of some poor soul who'd fallen into the pit prior.

Its skin, flesh, and organs had all been dissolved, leaving behind nothing but its bones. Next to it was a collection of armor, no doubt worn by the adventurer while still living. Looking away from their skeletal companion, they saw weapons of all kinds, swords and staves alike, either sticking up out of the ground or half-submerged in the boiling acid.

"Th-that's an adventurer…! Th-then all of these, too…?!"

Now that they were looking, they saw bones everywhere. Gleaming white bones. More than they could count. Belonging to who knew how many souls. It was clear that all of them had once been adventurers.

There were cracks and chips in some of the bones and skulls, as though something or other had bashed them in. There were even a few items of seemingly monster origin floating about—drops, perhaps.

Was this some sort of undocumented Dungeon gimmick? Here? In the safety point? Involving monsters, no less?

Lefiya's eyes watered at the rancid odor of melting flesh, confusion overtaking her thoughts…until Bell's trembling voice broke her from her trance.

"Miss Lefiya…look up," he whispered, features all but devoid of color.

"Huh?" She turned her gaze skyward.

Something was slowly peeling itself away from the fleshy walls of the hole, lifting its upper body…and enveloping them in its massive shadow.

"_____"

Suddenly, the true origin of the "lid" became clear.

As Lefiya and Bell looked up in terror, the monster hanging upside down from the top of the hole peered at them from its humanoid torso.

It was the only exception to the solid red of the hole, its skin a sickly shade of yellowish green. Its chest and abdomen, too, were colored in vibrant, venomous hues.

Instead of arms, it boasted two long, fat tentacles—feelers of sorts that dangled downward like quivering snakes. Its long lower half writhed and squirmed, attached to the wall like some kind of parasitic worm.

Its head consisted of nothing but a colossal eye and a strange crown-like organ floating around it. The eye itself was connected directly to its neck with the crown encircling it like the mane of a lion.

It was disgusting to look at, its coloring far different from that of the countless other monsters they'd fought.

"A…a new species…?" Bell's words quivered, the fear and dread palpable in his voice.

"It's one of those…brightly colored ones…!!" Lefiya exclaimed next to him as everything suddenly fell into place.

This "pitfall" they'd plunged into was none other than one of those monsters, the same as the carnivorous flowers and their roots—a brethren of the creatures born of the corrupted spirit—and its body was the pitfall itself!

If she had to guess, those Evils associates had planted it here as a security measure in order to keep whatever was past the Crystal

Grove, some all-important secret of theirs, away from prying eyes. It was a "trap monster" whose sole purpose was to eliminate any and all witnesses to their evil plan.

No doubt, the other adventurers who'd fallen prey to this "Guardian of the Forest" had either been trailing the Evils, similar to Lefiya and Bell, or had simply been in the wrong place at the wrong time. Completely ignorant, they'd been gobbled up by this repugnant creature, and their carcasses had been left to rot at the bottom of this pit.

"_____"

The creature's great eye spun around and around before centering itself on Lefiya and Bell.

Its next move was immediate. Both its feelers shot from its body straight toward the two adventurers.

""Gngh!!""

They leaped from their spots simultaneously.

The giant whips collided with the ground immediately behind them, straight into the middle of the acidic pool.

A massive wave of acid erupted upon the impact as the pit shuddered around them.

"Miss Lefiya!!"

"I am fine! Look after yourself!" Lefiya shouted back, one arm up to shield her eyes from the spraying acid.

They were soaked now, steam rising from their hair and clothes, but they'd somehow managed to avoid the attack. Still, it wasn't over yet, and the whips were quick to begin their second wave.

"Hngh!!"

Once again, the earth shook around them. The shock was enough to send the bones flying into the air with hollow clatters.

Though Lefiya just barely managed to evade the incoming attack, and the resulting rush of air and stone-rattling tremor were enough to make her blood run cold.

The sheer brute strength of this thing could give the monsters in the Dungeon's depths a run for their money. Even if the adventurers put all their efforts into defending themselves, their complete pulverization was only a matter of time. The elastic-like flexibility of the two tentacles didn't help matters, either—as long as they were stuck inside this hole, they were vulnerable. And the fact that the attacks were coming from straight overhead made defending against them a struggle, to say the least.

If this thing is here...it means...!

Lefiya's eyes narrowed as she stared at the trap monster above her, whose upper half alone was easily twice her size.

For the Evils to leave this kind of extraordinary creature here as a sentry meant that whatever it was they were hiding had to be of great importance.

She had to escape and let Finn and the others know.

I have to make it out of here alive...No! I have to kill this thing!

It was do or die now. There was no way she'd be able to escape without taking the body of that thing head-on. Or if there was, at least, she had no idea what it might be.

If they wanted to get out of here fast, their only choice was to destroy that creature's main body, as that was what was currently blocking their only way out.

Lefiya's fingers tightened around the grip of her magic staff, Forest's Teardrop.

"＿＿＿＿＿＿＿＿＿＿＿＿＿＿＿!!"

It was coming.

Its great eye goggled and whirled in ceaseless orbit, omniscient in its surveillance as it launched its two feelers at the adventurers.

Once again, it was aiming to kill.

"Hgh...gggnnnnn!!"

Bell was floundering, racing about wildly in his attempt to escape the oncoming attack.

He'd never seen this kind of monster before. The Guild hadn't even confirmed it. How was he supposed to defend himself against a monster he hadn't even known existed? Leaping about blindly, he narrowly avoided one attack after another, looking more and more like a rabbit in panic mode.

His sensational rate of growth aside, Bell Cranell hadn't actually seen many battles.

In fact, that same growth rate in some ways was actually an impediment—his lack of real combat experience exposing just how fragile he really was.

And somehow, as Lefiya watched him, giant beads of sweat leaking down his face, a sense of tranquility passed over her.

—The fact that this was an enemy she'd never faced before calmed her all the more.

She let the teachings of her mentors in *Loki Familia*, of Riveria, of Aiz, wash through her.

She knew what she was supposed to do upon first contact with a monster, to analyze and deal with it. She might not have the same level of perception as her first-tier adventurer peers, but it was more than nothing, and as the situation accelerated around her, she focused everything she had on understanding the creature in front of her.

Dodging attack after attack, girding herself against the pulsating shudders echoing around her, she studied the main body of the beast, focusing her elven eyes, which had originally made the elves "Archers of the Forest."

It was then, while scrutinizing the creature's great revolving eye, that she saw it.

"Watch where that thing is looking!"

"Huh?!"

"Its eye!! It turns in the direction it's about to attack!"

Bell's own eyes widened in startled realization as he immediately looked skyward.

That revolting eye was pointed directly at him. Studying the giant, naked orb, he was able to leap nimbly out of the way just in time as the massive tentacles slammed down beneath him.

They hit the exact spot he'd been occupying mere seconds earlier.

"I...I did it!" Bell exclaimed in jubilation after his magic-like prognosis left him unscathed.

"Those tentacles are its only weapon! Don't take your eyes off it!" Lefiya followed up before using the same method of foresight to sidestep another incoming tentacle.

"R-roger!"

The trap monster's appendages may have boasted incredible power and speed, but if that was the only trick it had up its sleeve, it made for an almost monotonous back and forth. So long as they could continue reading the creature's incoming attacks, they would at least be able to avoid any direct hits.

No longer cornered and fighting for their lives, they might actually have a chance to break the deadlock.

*Now to figure out how to attack that thing. If Miss Aiz was here, she'd simply jump off the wall to attack it directly...*Lefiya thought to herself, picturing the scene in her head.

Yes, she'd jump from wall to wall, ascending the hole like a lightning bolt in reverse, then *kerslash!!* It would be over.

Lefiya quickly shook herself from her thoughts.

If either of them was to try such a tactic, they'd surely be bludgeoned by one of those whips the moment they got close. *Stupid, stupid!* She mentally scolded herself. She had to change her way of thinking.

"I'm going to look for an opening and hit it with a spell! You focus all your efforts on attacking that wall!" she finally yelled, knowing the boy didn't have any long-range weapons of his own.

"Understood!"

The two of them sped off in opposite directions.

Unsheathing his onyx dagger, Bell launched himself immediately at the wall, dodging incoming whips as he unleashed slash after slash upon its fleshy pink surface. Heroic blue flashes cut through the air as he sliced at the enemy's insides.

—He really was fast.

Even as she focused on dodging attacks, Lefiya couldn't help the twinge of astonishment tugging at her.

As much as she hated it, his agility was top-notch—a fact she knew well thanks to their multiple games of tag. Even now, the way he was weaving in and out of the monster's attacks while unleashing furious slashes looked like a high-speed hit-and-run.

Despite only just leveling up, he was already fast enough that he'd been able to dodge the incoming tentacles' attacks even before Lefiya had given him the advice about following the enemy's gaze.

Thinking back now, Lefiya realized Aiz herself had praised the boy's ability to flee from danger back when she'd still been training him before the expedition.

Guilt began to whittle away at Lefiya's conscience—it was her fault Bell had gotten mixed up in this, after all—but in the end, all she could do was believe in the boy and focus on the battle at hand.

If I had to hazard a guess, this thing is just like those man-eating flowers...

The monster's outward appearance was actually quite similar to the femanoid creatures formed when that crystal-orb fetus parasitized other monsters. Perhaps this was another member of that thing's advanced army, just like the flowers?

Both the femanoids they'd battled on the fiftieth and eighteenth floors were massive, on par with floor bosses, and their power had been well over that of a Level 5. This trap monster couldn't be far behind in either aspect.

Its colossal size alone, which placed it in the "superlarge monster" category, gave it the potential of at least a Level 4.

!!

The tentacles were coming at them more aggressively now, the thing no doubt angered that it couldn't catch its prey.

They swung downward, destroyed everything, then lunged forward. The relentless storm of elephantine whips was becoming harder and harder for Lefiya and Bell to dodge. The swords, axes, and shields that had been stuck in the ground at their feet were tossed about with a wild vengeance, almost as though giving life to the lingering regrets of their owners. Though the acid had already completely dissolved much of the weaponry, the upper-tier arms of silver and mythril still retained their original forms.

Lefiya dodged these additional incoming projectiles before grimacing in pain—her shoes had practically melted away at this point, steam rising up from her feet as the acid ate away at her skin.

Knowing that a part of her was slowly and surely disappearing entirely was enough to make her insides scream.

Their one consolation was that this acid took considerable time to do its dirty work.

Its strength was nothing compared to the corrosive acid the caterpillar monsters secreted.

Whether its giant structure was at fault or not, the creature had two primary features—its main body and the hole itself—that seemed to have different functions: predation and pursuit. As Lefiya took all this into account, her past experiences facing off against enhanced species such as creatures and demi-spirits weighing in on her diagnosis, she couldn't help but think that the creature itself wasn't fully developed.

"Gngh…!"

At the same time, Bell's flurry of countless attacks at the thing's inner walls didn't seem to be getting him anywhere.

His beloved onyx knife itself was doing fine, neither melting nor clouding at the repeated slashes of the acid-secreting flesh, and the cuts it left were many and deep.

But the walls were too thick.

If they weren't even able to make a solid dent in the surrounding walls, it certainly wasn't going to have any effect on the thing above them.

The thing had yet to show any signs of pain or annoyance at the scratches Bell was making on its pink inner walls.

It's not even flinching…! Lefiya thought to herself as she bit down hard on her lip.

While she hadn't been expecting anything revolutionary, if the boy's attacks could have slowed the creature even a little, she might have been able to find an opening to unleash one of her spells. It appeared, however, that things weren't going to be that easy.

This hole really was not only a luring trap but an ensnaring prison, too.

Their only choice, then, was to attack it directly—the magic stone hidden somewhere within its chest.

But the problem with that is...

...whether or not she could dodge the incoming tentacles long enough to pull off a spell.

Even if she used Concurrent Casting, the bit of focus she had to devote to the chant itself severely lowered her reaction and response time, to the point where no amount of reading into the enemy's movements was going to stop her from being sliced to pieces by those whips.

The closed-in space with limited room to escape didn't help matters any, either.

And that wasn't even getting into the fact that nine times out of ten, these vibrantly colored monsters tended to respond to magic. The instant she started casting her spell, the incoming attacks that had been, until now, divided evenly between Bell and her would all be focused straight on her.

While she would have liked to coordinate something together with Bell, she wasn't about to hold her breath with such a hastily formed dyad as theirs. And even she wasn't about to do something as cruel as force a Level-2 third-tier to act as a wall for her against this kind of enemy.

No, she'd simply have to do it on her own.

Bracing herself, she began preparing for her chant.

"_____"

It was then that it happened.

The relentless wave of attacks coming at them simply—paused.

Lefiya and Bell both stopped short, looking up at the motionless creature with identical expressions of incredulity.

Its giant eye was still rolling about, back and forth between the two of them.

Upside down and hanging from the ceiling, it gazed upon its nimble prey.

Then.

The crown-like organ around its head began to glow a brilliant blue.

"Huh—?!" Bell's confusion escaped his lips as Lefiya found herself unable to move.

Something bad was about to happen. Something very bad. But this realization came too late.

From the glowing blue crown encircling its eye came a devastating wave of high-frequency sound.

"*Huuuuuuaaaaaaaaaaaaaaaaaaaaaaaaaaaahhhh———————!!*"

The noise was deafening, splitting their eardrums, and all Lefiya and Bell could do was scream as their eyes nearly popped free of their sockets.

"""————————————————————————————Gnh!!"""

It was a monster cry, similar to those of bad bats and sirens and capable of restricting adventurers' movements.

Only this cry was incredible, stronger and fiercer than the cry of any ordinary monster.

The shriek had enough destructive force to rob even upper-class adventurers of consciousness, rendering Lefiya and Bell incapable of movement in less than an instant.

They fell to their knees with sloshy *thud*s, the otherworldly cry robbing them of all balance.

!!

The creature didn't miss its chance.

Its two tentacles, primed and ready, went screeching toward its prey.

"————————"

Their target: Bell.

The world hazy around them, Lefiya's breath stopped in her throat as Bell froze before the imminent attack.

A Level 2 up against what could easily be considered a Level 4.

A direct hit meant certain death.

A one-hit kill.

Lefiya screamed.

"*Run!!*"

And Bell did, his body ready to put his emergency evasive maneuvers to the test. But it was too late.

The two tentacles streaked toward him, slicing through the air in an instant, and as the boy kicked off the ground, his foot came in contact with one of the armaments that had been sticking out of the acid, sending it flying.

—A shield!

A parting gift from one of the adventurers consumed by the creature, the large silver shield somersaulted through the air, Lefiya's eyes widening as its path sent it directly in front of the oncoming tentacles.

A second later...

...an earth-shattering noise shook the world around them, almost like an explosion going off, and Bell's body was launched away like a bullet.

"Gaggghh!"

He zoomed through the air.

The phenomenal impact of the tentacles with the shield sent him careering into the walls of flesh.

The collision reopened the wound on his head in a spray of red-hot blood. His body peeled away from the wall, plunging into the pool of acid with a splash.

He stayed there, motionless, white steam rising from his frame as the acid ate away at his skin.

......

The deafening cry coming from the trap monster's crown fizzled into nothingness.

Then, one of its tentacles extended like a long spear, shooting straight toward the boy to land the final blow.

However—

"——*Unleashed beam of light, limbs of the holy tree!!*"

—Lefiya was ready.

In an attempt to thwart the attack, she wove her spell.

The magic circle formed beneath her feet, proudly announcing her presence, golden light rising from the acid's surface with a rippling shudder.

The reaction was immediate. The tentacle shooting toward Bell veered sharply in its trajectory.

Rolling its entire body over, the trap monster changed its target. This time, it was pointed straight at Lefiya.

"You are the master archer!"

!!

Lefiya took off at a dash, her voice soaring as she fled the rampaging set of tentacles.

It was the most desperate Concurrent Casting she'd ever performed—controlling her web of magic as she flew through the confined space of the hole, all the while continuing her song.

"Loose your arrows, fairy archers—!"

The whips rushed at her, cutting through the air, the rushes of wind in their wake slashing at her battle clothes. Even as her feet moved at a frenzied clip, she never took her eyes away from the creature's single eye. She used everything Filvis had taught her—to throw aside her defenses, to continue even as her body was battered—simply dodging everything she could as she read into the enemy's movements and continued her chant.

Her insides were boiling hot as if to fuel her mad rush, sweat pouring down her forehead and all across her skin.

!

As she clutched her staff, as she wove her spell, as she dodged attack after attack by naught but a hair's breadth, the trap monster moved its head.

Then that same light, that terrifying blue light, erupted from its crown.

"Huuuuuaaaaaaaaaaaaaggggghhhhh————————!!"

"Gnngh—*pierce, arrow of accuracy!!*"

Lefiya raised her voice, face distorting as she competed with the incoming wave of high-frequency sound.

Just as she completed the spell, however, the tentacle she thought she'd evaded changed its course, curling like a snake and latching onto her left wrist.

"Oh n—!!"

Suddenly she was up in the air, hanging by her left arm, before getting forcefully bashed against the wall.

"Guuuuhhh!!"

The air was knocked out of her.

Chant interrupted, the magic circle disappeared from beneath her feet.

The trap monster's other tentacle was quick to descend, mercilessly shrieking toward her as she continued to hang helplessly in the air.

Ah—

The color drained from her face at the sight of the cyclops's whip filling her vision.

In that moment, her mind flashed back to a gold and silver gleam— her golden-haired, golden-eyed swordswoman, when Aiz had rescued her from those carnivorous flowers.

But in the next moment...

"—Yooooooooooooouuuuuuuuuu bastaaaaaaaaaaaard!!"

...a white shadow raced toward her...

"Huh?!"

...before slamming itself into the tentacle on its collision course with Lefiya's body.

The white shadow—Bell—swung the great ax in his hands with every drop of strength he had left in him and brought it down on the massive whip.

The blade struck with a jarring jolt.

?!

Impact sending it off course, the rushing tentacle missed Lefiya's body by a mere celch's width.

Lefiya held her breath, shocked by the fact that she was still alive, as she felt the shock waves from the point-blank attack. Bell touched ground for only a moment before leaping back up with his ax flying.

He sank the blade into the thick tentacle curled around Lefiya's wrist, blood gushing from the wound as he severed it whole.

"...Y-you..."

Free from the creature's grasp and having fallen to the pit's floor, Lefiya looked up at the boy standing before her.

His back was to her, as though he was placing himself between the enemy and her.

A thin white mist rose from his body as the acid continued to eat at his skin, the large mythril ax, a nameless weapon of dwarven use, clenched tightly in his hands.

Blood from the wound on his head stained his back and shoulders, but even still, his eyes never left the creature staring down at them from above.

!!

A creature that appeared very angry now, its one eye bloodshot and glowering as its severed tentacle squirmed like a decapitated snake.

The glow returned to its crown. This time it was going in for the kill.

NOT good! Lefiya's heart screamed at her as the monster howled anew.

Bell, however, wasn't about to let it happen. Raising his right arm—

"Firebolt!!"

—he fired his own blast.

Scarlet tendrils of lightning—no, of fire—shot forth from his hand.

For just a moment, time seemed to stop. As Lefiya watched, the blinding-fast bolt of sparkling flames shot toward the creature, shattering its crown of light before it even had a chance to unleash its cry.

"_____*Gngh?!*"

Again and again the fiery tendrils hit, nine in total.

Every single one of them was a direct hit, completely disintegrating the trap monster's crown.

The crown exploded in a flurry of sparks, abruptly halting its high-pitched scream.

He...he didn't even have to chant?!

Lefiya couldn't believe her eyes. She'd never seen such a thing, never even heard of such a thing.

A chant-less, instant spell.

And not only that, but he could fire them one after another.

——*Is this some kind of joke?!* she almost found herself screaming, in complete disbelief as a mage.

"Miss Lefiya! Your spell!!" Bell howled in between haggard breaths.

Lefiya shook herself from her daze, head snapping up to see that vibrantly colored creature right above her, flames raking its body in a fiery inferno.

Its crown continued to blaze, but even through its anguished cries, its one great eye was still pointed at Lefiya and Bell. It was enraged.

Bell readied himself as the trap monster's fury swelled in tangible waves around them.

His own magic might not have been powerful enough to defeat that thing, but he was going to protect Lefiya and give her all the time it took for her to pull off her own spell. That much was clear from his stance.

Even if his fingers were crushed beneath their shield, even if his body was rent limb from limb, he was going to keep swinging that ax, and he was going to protect her.

"I…I hate you…"

It happened without warning.

The words simply fell from her mouth.

How could he be so cool?

How could he cheat with magic like that?

How could he monopolize Aiz, have her waiting on him, completely ignorant of his own place?!

And yet.

"And yet…I believe in you."

He was an adventurer.

And she—she was a mage.

She had faith in those rubellite eyes gazing at her from over his shoulder.

"—I'm ready."

Raising her staff, Forest's Teardrop, she called forth a giant magic circle beneath her feet.

"—————————————————*Gnnh!!*"

The trap monster responded immediately and started moving toward Lefiya, drawn in by the colossal source of magic.

Their last stand had begun.

The boy with his ax and the girl with her song.

"Unleashed beam of light, limbs of the holy tree."

The moment Lefiya took off running, chant on her lips, the two tentacles gave chase.

Bell, however, quickly closed in on the elephantine whips, reading the enemy's movements and leaping forward to bash them from the side as they came in for their attack.

He gave it everything he had, gritting his teeth as he chopped away, feet never faltering.

"You are the master archer."

The trap monster had made one grave mistake.

No, perhaps *mistake* wasn't the proper word, for it had only allowed an innate weakness to be exposed.

Its tendency to react immediately to any and all magic *no matter the circumstances.*

Had the creature thought to focus its efforts on Bell, currently barely hanging on for dear life, rather than Lefiya and her chanting, the battle would have been over before it started. And once her human shield, Bell, was gone, Lefiya would be quick to follow.

By acting as a decoy as she cast her spell, however, she allowed Bell plenty of time to execute his skills in complete safety.

It was the same defensive method the Sword Princess had hammered into her—that she should deflect the enemy's attacks to the side.

Though Bell couldn't hope to take that creature head-on, what with their difference in potential, he could sneak in some attacks so long as Lefiya distracted its tentacles. Again and again he gave chase, using his lightning-fast feet and mighty ax to forcibly direct the tentacles' path away from the mage.

It was a feat made possible only by both his evasive skills and Lefiya's Concurrent Casting.

There in that hole in the earth, the labors and toils of those two adventurers both trained by the same girl came together and bore fruit.

"Loose your arrows, fairy archers—!"

The words came between the relentless attacks.

As she neared the end of her chant, her magic power rising sharply, the trap monster increased its efforts, throwing everything it had at the mage to stop her song.

But Bell held it back, ax flying as he kept the two flailing tentacles in check.

"Gnnngh!"

He launched himself at the swinging tendril. Though his attack came from the side, the shock was still enough to send his body flying, mythril ax drawing an arc across the air as it sailed away.

Still, however, he had managed to protect her.

The strike that had previously been heading straight toward Lefiya instead grazed her long golden hair, colliding with the fleshy wall behind her.

As the world shook with a ferocious tremor around her, Lefiya's voice rose to meet the cacophony head-on.

"—Pierce, arrow of accuracy!"

The chant was complete.

In the center of that great hole, directly below the trap monster, Lefiya thrust her staff to the sky.

And in that moment, the red world around them shone a brilliant, vivid gold.

She cried out the name of the spell, magic circle overtaking the entirety of the hole.

"Arcs Ray!!"

There was a burst of light.

Then the gleaming flash shot straight upward at a blinding speed.

The trap monster attempted to flee, withdrawing its tentacles and wedging itself into the passage above, but it was no use.

Its fate was sealed.

The phenomenal Mind built up within that single blast tore

through its tentacles before landing a direct hit on the creature's main body.

"————————————————————*Gguuwwwwaahhh!!*"

Its lower half, partially assimilated into the wall itself, writhed and squirmed like a snake as the blinding flash propelled its body upward.

Then, it collided with the lid of the hole, still closed tight above them, with an absolutely deafening crash.

The pillar of light, however, was brought to a screeching halt.

"It stopped the attack?!"

The creature's upper half remained with the stubs of its arms outstretched. The hole's red lid was worn down from the incoming magic light but still very much intact. That thing had absorbed the brunt of the attack, keeping it from bursting through the top of the pitfall.

Lefiya was shocked at what she was seeing.

A strangely colored monster above their heads and its two-part body, each with its own separate function.

An "adventurer's prison" keeping them trapped.

The lengths it took to keep their sole way out from being opened.

And the specialized magic resistance it took to do so—

Her thoughts ran wild at the attributes the creature must have possessed—attributes that made it every bit the "trap monster" it was.

But Lefiya didn't care. Lefiya didn't care one single bit, her eyes flashing with a determined gleam.

It was a competition between monster and magic—erupting with light.

The creature's greenish-yellow skin curled and burned as it absorbed the incoming magic, its scream of anguish swallowed up by the roar of her light blast. The magic stone at the tip of her Forest's Teardrop glowed with a brilliant pale blue, infusing her spell with more and more of her Mind.

As Lefiya increased her output, injecting everything she had into that beam of energy, the giant charred eye of the beast turned toward her in incensed fury.

Not more than an instant later, the entire hole roared.

"Wha—?!"

The walls of flesh began to swell.

Like tumors, almost, one after another, giant lumps began to billow out from the pink surface with a ghastly bubbling hiss, closing in on Lefiya from all four sides. They pushed the pool of acid with them, the liquid forming a wave that yanked and swirled at her feet.

—It aims to crush us?!

Knowing its own demise was only a matter of time, it had decided to take them down with it—by setting loose its own body.

It would destroy itself, and the hole around them, crushing them in the process.

Lefiya's body grew hot. Blazingly hot. All the magic power she'd accumulated inside her in her attempt to blast the creature (and the lid) out of the way was now, all of a sudden, getting forced back onto her as the thing overhead let out a crazed roar of cataclysmic obliteration.

The walls quickly swallowed up the carcasses of the other adventurers around them.

Lefiya's features contorted into something unrecognizable.

When suddenly…

Ching ching.

"—Huh?"

…an entirely out-of-place chime tickled her eardrums.

Unable to resist, she turned around, only to see the boy, wounds and all, rising to his feet.

His right hand glowed with a pale-white light, building and building as he summoned the particles to him.

"…Gngh!"

He was limping toward her, dragging his battered body as he waded through the pool of acid, already up to his knees.

He didn't stop until he was right next to her. Lefiya was still directing her magic skyward even through her shock, and then he extended his hand, glowing white ball joining her staff, still raised high.

"I'll...join you...!" He gritted his teeth, left hand coming up to support his wrist.

His cannon was primed and ready, and Lefiya's eyes widened before she turned her gaze upward.

Together with the boy, she directed a glare of death at the enemy overhead—*We're not going down here!*—before calling forth her magic power with everything she had.

Her light gleamed brighter.

Before being joined by the pure-white brilliance of the boy's collected particles.

A bell chimed.

Then, twenty seconds later, he pulled the trigger.

"Firebolt!!"

The brilliant white light burst from his hand.

"_____"

The massive, crackling fire tore through the white particles.

Above them, the trap monster's body went white, bathed in the radiance of this second attack.

And this time, as the two gleams overlapped, as the fiery lightning tore into the creature's body, the imprisoning lid of the hole overhead shattered.

The trap monster dissolved into the blinding flash, leaving no trace behind.

"Gnh!!"

As the monster's agonizing death cry melded noiselessly into the din, the pillar of lightning shot all the way up toward the sky.

It blasted through the crust of the earth, through the roof of trees, filling Lefiya's eyes with the breathtaking view of the crystalline night sky overhead. The path had been opened.

At the same time, the sheet of rock that made up the Dungeon's

floor convulsed with a mighty jolt as it began to collapse without the monster that had been parasitizing it.

Lefiya picked up the spent boy's body from the ground, bent her knees as far as they would bend, then leaped out of the hole.

Her Level-3 leg strength propelling her up the great height, she sprang off the falling rocks to send her the rest of the way, escaping back into the Under Resort above.

"What the hell was that—?!"

"Is that magic?!"

The two Amazons shouted as all of *Loki Familia* sprang to its feet.

The sudden beacon of light that shot out of the forest quickly drew the attention of everyone on the eighteenth floor.

The single column of radiant light was visible from the great tree in the center of the plains, from Rivira on its island in the lake, and even from *Loki Familia*'s camp.

The group was just finishing up their dinner when the spectacle unfolded, Tiona's and Tione's shouts leading them to leap into the trees for a better view.

As the brilliant white flash of entangled beams struck the crystal-coated ceiling, the resulting explosion sent the monsters below it into a frenzy. The cacophonous array of frightened squawks echoed all throughout the eighteenth floor.

"It came from the forest…to the east? What's over there?" Tione murmured beneath her breath.

"You don't think it could be Lefiya…do you?" Tiona posed as her eyes scanned the scene from above. She saw Finn and the other elites emerge from their tent, eyes narrowing at the giant column of light; she saw *Loki Familia*'s lower-level members bustling and clamoring; and she even saw Hestia and the others in her group, dumbfounded as to what was going on, but nowhere in all that commotion did she see Lefiya.

And certainly, that kind of magic power did seem compatible with the elven mage.

In fact, she was the first person who came to mind, especially given how they hadn't seen her since she'd run off chasing that white-haired boy not too long ago.

"Ngh!"

All these thoughts flying around her mind, Aiz suddenly took off, dashing from the camp without warning.

"Huh? Aiz!!"

But Tiona's voice fell on deaf ears. The swordswoman was already well out of sight.

The pillar of light had faded. In its place, giant chunks of crystal fell from the ceiling like glimmering blue rain.

It was toward the source of that crystal rain that Aiz ran—her sword at the ready.

Smoke billowed upward in great, heavy clouds.

Deep within that mighty forest, it looked almost as though lightning had struck.

Many of the crystal pillars that had made up the stone circle were cracked or toppled to the side, evidence of the terrific shock that had shaken the earth around them. Directly above the scene, hidden by the forest's mesh of trees and branches, a giant round hole had formed in the ceiling, one crystalline chunk after another dropping to the ground below and shattering like glass.

"Haah…haah…Hey, are you all right?!"

"…Y-yeah…"

They were pressed shoulder to shoulder, breath haggard as the blue-crystal snow fell down around them.

Having barely escaped with their lives, they were now kneeling down in the grass a short distance from the collapsed hole. Though both appeared considerably worse for wear, the boy's body was more visibly fatigued than Lefiya's, the mage still having some fight left in her despite her ragged breathing.

That final attack had seemingly consumed the last of Bell's strength, and his wounds were many—the reopened gash on the back of his head, as well as the burns all over his skin from its exposure to the acid. In fact, the only part of him not charred was his salamander-wool linens, still remarkably unscathed.

Lefiya had left her pouch of potions back at camp—an apparent lapse of judgment on her part—so she had no choice but to simply hoist the boy up by his shoulder and attempt to drag him away.

"What's going on here?!"

It was then that the voice called out from behind her.

She turned around with a start, only to see a pair of men racing out of the forest toward her from the direction of the Dungeon's easternmost wall. They wore large robes, head protectors adorning their foreheads, and hoods covering the better part of their faces. It was the very same Evils associates Lefiya and Bell had been trailing before they'd gotten into this mess.

As they caught sight of Lefiya and Bell in the middle of the crumbling Crystal Grove, their surprise was evident.

"Thousand Elf? Then you're...*Loki Familia*?!"

"You defeated Venenthes?!"

It didn't take more than a single look for them to ascertain the situation—that the two adventurers had followed them, fallen into their trap, and then taken down the trap monster waiting for them inside.

Their surprise turned quickly to irritation, scowls tangible even from within their heavy robes.

"Damn you...! Quickly! Release the violas!" the more emphatic of the two shouted, and his partner dived into the nearby brush.

The situation could not have gotten any worse. Someone somewhere was laughing at them. Even Bell had tensed next to her. The dire turn their escape had taken was obvious.

As if on cue, one greenish tentacle after another began poking itself out of the surrounding greenery, crawling toward them fast.

"Hngh...?!"

Lefiya heard the metallic sound of first one cage, then another, then another being opened, and soon, she and Bell were completely surrounded. Their faces paled at the circle of carnivorous flowers caging them in.

There were so many of them. Ten, at least.

They lifted their great crooked necks, tentacles writhing and squirming like snakes and effectively cutting off their every escape route.

"This is where you die, adventurer scum!" shouted the robed figures as they quickly vacated the premises to keep from getting caught up in the mix. The moment they left, the violas opened their buds in sync, revealing their vibrantly colored petals and ghastly jaws.

Heaping gobs of saliva dripped from their fangs onto the scattered bits of crystal littering the grass below.

"Gnngh...?!"

Lefiya was already well past spent from their earlier fight against the trap monster, and she still had Bell to worry about. The boy was scarcely able to move next to her.

The situation was truly dire, to the point where her own life was starting to flash before her eyes.

If she could just get Bell away from here. Somehow. She was the one who'd gotten him mixed up in this, after all.

She made the decision right then and there that she wasn't going to go down quietly.

As the ring of man-eating flowers slowly closed in on her, liable to pounce at a moment's notice, she tightened her grip on her beloved staff, still holding Bell aloft to her side.

"—Uuuuuuooooooooooooowwwwwwaaaaaaaaaahhhhhhhh!!"

One of the flowers roared, preparing to launch itself upon them.

Until a sudden whirling storm howled its way onto the battlefield.

"Gwwuooogh?!"

"—What?!"

The flower was cut off mid-leap, quickly mowed down by the gale and flying sideways into the surrounding flowers.

One thunderous boom after another shook the environs. Lefiya and Bell could only look on in stupefied wonder, still primed and ready for their own attacks, as this new assailant landed on the ground in front of them.

—*Miss Aiz?*

But no, the figure that appeared before them was not Lefiya's beloved swordswoman—but a long-caped figure, fabric rustling in the storm's wake.

"I thought I heard something…Are these the new species?"

The figure wore lightweight battle clothes, a long wooden sword readied in their right hand.

Their face was completely obscured within the deep recesses of their hood.

As this lone adventurer stood with their back to them, protecting them from the bright green threat, Lefiya's pupils dilated in surprise.

Lefiya was sure she'd seen this person before. Last night. Among those in the rescue party—

"—The masked…adventurer?"

Her lips parted with the words just as Bell, next to her, spoke up with a raspy voice.

"Miss Lyu…"

Their reinforcement, who'd dashed in gallantly to save them, now stood facing the swarm of carnivorous flowers head-on, an impenetrable fortress.

She flourished her wooden sword, the same one that had sent the mighty creatures flying only moments earlier, with a warrior's will.

"Don't move, elf. Stay there with Mister Cranell." The voice that called out to her was authoritative, awe-inspiring, and Lefiya quickly nodded.

"O-okay!"

No sooner had the words left her lips than the wind picked up with a sudden *whoosh*.

The figure was gone in an instant, kicking off the ground with an audible *slash* that cut through the grass—the flower that had been in front of her bucked.

With that single wooden sword, she sent the colossal beast flying, the same as she had earlier. Lefiya didn't even have time to act surprised. The masked adventurer drew a giant circle with her sword that uprooted every single one of the flowers in her immediate surroundings. The resulting crystal-clear *sheeeen* rang in her ears.

The throng of abominable flowers that had been pressing in on Lefiya and Bell from all sides was launched away in one fell swoop.

So...so fast!!

Lefiya found herself rooted to the spot as she watched the figure dance like a hurricane. Even Lefiya's Level-3 vision wasn't enough to keep up with her. The flowers, too, were at a loss, squealing in agony as the figure slipped deftly through the swarm of countless flying tentacles and landed another direct hit. They crashed into the crystal pillars still scattered about the area, their large bodies taking beating after beating against the hard rock.

It was so fast. So intense. Both Lefiya and Bell found themselves at a loss for words.

"This...this is..."

As did the two Evils associates.

Watching the battle play out from their spot a short distance away, they could only bite their tongues in astonishment at the unprecedented one-sided battle taking place before them.

"...These things."

Again and again the masked adventurer slammed the flowers with everything she had, but no matter how many times they flew backward, they'd just give angered roars and pick themselves up, charging at her for another round.

Even through the minimal contact her sword made with their skin, she could tell it was tough—infuriatingly so. And no matter how much power she put behind her attacks, she couldn't seem to make a mark in that thick layer of skin. A look of admiration crossed her face.

Lefiya was quick to notice. "S-simply hitting those things won't do anything! You have to cut them!" she shouted, offering the only advice she could give. And then, fascinated by the adventurer's sheer speed and intensity, reminiscent of the Sword Princess, as well as the elven ears beneath her rescuer's hood, she tossed out one more suggestion. "Magic works, too!"

The effects were immediate.

The adventurer pulled out a small *tachi*, using it to cut through the flowers' tentacles, then narrowed her clear blue eyes—beginning her chant.

"—Distant sky above the forest. Limitless stars set into an eternal night."

She was Concurrent Casting.

Lefiya's eyes widened as wide as they would go.

The high-level magic power quickly drew the attention of all ten violas. They came at her all at once in a storm of roars and tentacles. But she parried every one of them, cutting them down, flinging them back, continuing her mad dash, never once letting her sonorous voice falter as it continued its song.

"Listen to my feeble voice and grant the protection of starlight. Bestow the light of mercy upon those who have abandoned you."

Attack, move, evade, chant. Together with her defensive maneuvers, which made for five different actions, each of them carried out with the utmost of celerity. Which was the most impressive part of all—that despite the chant, her astounding speed never slowed in the slightest.

The shock Lefiya felt was immeasurable.

The first person she could think of who even came close to this level of skill as a magic swordswoman was Filvis. But even Filvis's spells were short, not more than a single phrase, and quite unlike the long chant this girl was performing now. Even despite the lack of a magic circle, Lefiya could tell she was planning something big—a high-powered blast that would take everything out.

There was a difference when it came to Concurrent Casters and magic swordsmen.

Mostly in the form of the level of magic they could produce, something that mostly came down to the presence of a magic circle.

Concurrent Casters lived in the advanced or mid-guard, and their magic was their sole weapon. Magic swordsmen, on the other hand, were fighters specialized in magic to the point where they could take on a number of mages' abilities and command the front lines single-handedly. Mages like Lefiya and Riveria both belonged to the former group—back-line mages who'd learned the art of Concurrent Casting, making them mobile fortresses.

All of this meant that, strictly speaking, the adventurer in front of her now was not a magic swordswoman.

In fact, she was another entity entirely, different from those like Lefiya who lived on the back lines—an elven warrior.

Then...then that would make her even stronger than Miss Filvis. Th-than Lady Riveria even...!!

The precision of the masked adventurer's Concurrent Casting was far more exact, far speedier, and far less risky than that of a pure back-line mage such as Riveria.

And yet, no. It was simply that this elf was more used to this sort of chanting.

There was no telling how many times she'd practiced.

While on the front line with no one to protect her, her song the only path to victory, she flourished her sword as she sang her omnipotent melody.

"Come, wind of winds, wandering traveler of the ages."

While so much of this elf reminded Lefiya of Aiz, there was still one outstanding difference between them.

The difference of sheer magic firepower, the ability to annihilate all enemies in a single instant, rather than simply taking them on one by one in hand-to-hand combat.

The scale of the magic she was casting now, the length of the chant she rattled off like nothing, was entirely unsuited for use in the advanced guard and could easily rival the magic of any upper-class mage.

It was almost as though someone had taken Lefiya and Aiz and merged them together to make a mobile fortress specialized in pure speed.

"Across the skies, through the fields, faster than any, farther than all."

Lefiya found herself at a complete and total loss for words. Truly, even a first-tier adventurer would find themselves taken aback by the Concurrent Casting taking place here. The elven warrior was single-handedly gathering the entire swarm of enemies together in front of her as if it was nothing.

In fact, even Bell was beyond impressed, not a single hitch in her song as her dance of storms continued.

"Light of stardust, tear my enemies asunder!"

And like that, the spell was complete.

With those final words, the masked adventurer jumped backward, putting distance between the flowers and herself.

Pointing her wooden sword at the giant swarm, she began summoning hundreds of thousands of massive light particles, all of them surrounding her, all of them heeding her call.

"Luminous Wind!!"

The stardust erupted in a brilliant green storm.

It was an image not unlike one of Lefiya's own spells, Fusillade Fallarica—a mass collection of particles all launched at once, incinerating everything along their wide path.

The teeming throng of man-eating flowers still coming at the girl was quick to get swallowed up by the burst of light.

"————————————————————*Guuuwaaaah?!*"

One explosion. Then another. Then ten, twenty, thirty, too many to count.

It was a direct hit. The searing volley carved into their bodies and detonated with a brilliant flash and an explosion of petals and tentacles. Not even their vibrantly colored magic stones survived the blast, shattering instantly and turning the monsters' flesh to ash.

The horrific ground-shaking eruption, the mountain of piled-up corpses, the gallons of smoke rising from the ashes—Lefiya and Bell had to hold on to each other for support as their faces twitched in horror.

"...Perhaps that was a bit too much," the girl responsible for the carnage murmured almost ironically as she scanned the surrounding trees.

© Kiyotaka Haimura

Her sky-blue eyes narrowed in on where the two hidden Evils associates were frantically attempting to make their escape.

It would seem they were all out of tricks. The battle, then, had come to an end.

Cape still fluttering, the girl sheathed her small wooden sword and *tachi*.

Then, her long boots whistling through the grass, she made her way straight toward Lefiya and Bell.

"Ah! Th-thank you so much for saving us…I, uh…You are…?"

"Later. You both need medical assistance first." The girl responded to her kin's openmouthed stupor after only a quick glance at both of their conditions. While Bell obviously needed help, Lefiya, too, sported a number of nasty-looking cuts and bruises.

The adventurer immediately went to work healing them both.

She sat Bell down first. The boy didn't fight it, letting himself drop to the grass, though keeping his mouth strangely quiet, almost as though unsure whether or not he should say the girl's name out loud with Lefiya present.

"I, erm…"

"You shouldn't move, Mister Cranell," the girl advised, getting down on one knee before raising her right hand toward the boy's face.

"Distant song above the forest. Nostalgic melody of life."

It was a different chant this time.

"Impart your healing upon those who seek your grace."

Identical looks of disbelief crossed Lefiya's and Bell's faces.

"Noah Heal."

A healing spell, just as they'd expected.

Soft, mottled light, almost like the sun through the trees, washed over Bell's body, closing up the deep wound on his head, as well as the cuts littering his face.

The warm light radiating from her palm healed his every scratch, his every bruise, his every acid burn, one after another.

"You…you can use healing magic, too…?" Bell asked, still in awe.

"Yes. Though its use is limited, as it cannot rival potions in its potency," she explained.

It was true—the Mind she was consuming now, as well as its effect, was considerably less than the attack magic she'd cast earlier, and nowhere near that of a healer's.

Lefiya, herself, couldn't help but feel a bit insecure, both as an adventurer and as a fellow magic-wielding elf. This jack-of-all-trades put her and her single-minded attack magic to shame. Even still, once the girl was finished with Bell, Lefiya didn't hesitate to allow the same to be done to her.

Soon, both adventurers were free from injury, and their melted, charred skin was as good as new.

Once he'd been given a bit of magic potion to complete the treatment, Bell got to his feet with a wobble, still slightly light-headed.

Lefiya, too, followed suit, fully prepared to ask the adventurer all the questions she'd wanted to earlier. However—

"—Well then, Mister Cranell...While I don't know exactly what happened here, I can't say that I'm not disappointed." The elf shot him a look of reproach.

"Oh..." Bell mumbled, wincing at the stern glare directed at him from under the other girl's hood.

"If memory serves me correctly, I delivered you safely back to camp not more than a few hours ago, yes? When you were running around lost in the forest."

"I...I'm sorry...!!"

"I had hoped you would have learned how dangerous the forest is at night," she continued, lecturing him now on the perils of wandering around the forest alone. Bell, in turn, let his head hang with a shrug, looking very much like a young boy being scolded by an older neighborhood kid.

A single glance was all it took to understand their relationship.

"W-wait! Please!"

But then.

Lefiya quickly interjected.

"It's my fault. Everything...everything is my fault! I was the one who...who dragged him into this mess!"

"..."

"He's done nothing wrong, so...so please, my sister. Don't misunderstand," she continued, looking straight past Bell in his surprise to meet the gaze of her kin. And then, despite considerable hesitation, despite her struggle to say it: "...He. He saved me," she finished, the words ringing clear and true.

It went without saying that she was at fault for involving him in her investigation of the two Evils associates, and if it hadn't been for Bell, she wasn't even sure she'd have escaped from that trap monster with her life.

As much as she didn't want to admit it, he'd saved her...and she was thankful for his protection.

Holding back her urge to grit her teeth, she admitted her own fault—and appealed on his behalf.

It was quiet for a moment as the masked adventurer simply listened in silence.

Then a small "Heh" sounded beneath the other adventurer's hood, and Lefiya could imagine her smile.

"You don't know how happy it makes me to meet another elf like you," she responded, voice filled with delight. The ability to lay down one's pride and admit one's own faults was something decidedly un-elven, after all.

Lefiya felt her cheeks grow warm at the sincere praise.

After a moment, the other girl turned toward Bell, lightly nodding.

"I apologize, then, Mister Cranell, for it appears I spoke too soon."

"N-no, it's, uh...I-I mean, it's still partly my fault..." Bell brought a hand to the back of his head sheepishly at the adventurer's apology.

Lefiya, on the other hand, while relieved that the misunderstanding had been cleared up...couldn't help but notice that the other girl's voice, the way she held herself...it all looked very familiar. In fact, she could have sworn she'd seen someone with that same exact disposition and build at a certain bar back in Orario—a thought that wouldn't seem to let her go, almost like a small bone that had gotten itself lodged in her throat and refused to go down.

Just as it was really starting to drive her crazy, she heard a sudden swish of branches from behind her—and a certain golden-haired, golden-eyed swordswoman dropped down from the trees above.

"Lefiya!"

"Miss Aiz?!" Lefiya whirled around in surprise at the other girl's entrance.

Aiz's gaze softened with relief at seeing both Lefiya and Bell unharmed, her eyes flicking immediately toward the masked adventurer.

"Sword Princess..." the girl murmured, hiding her face within her deep hood.

Kicking up and off the grass, she dropped back a few paces as Lefiya and Bell both gave a start.

"I assume you'll be fine now. I've other things to attend to, so I'll take my leave here. If you'll excuse me," she finished, before disappearing in the opposite direction from which Aiz was approaching.

Lefiya, Bell, and Aiz all watched in silence as she vanished into the forest.

"Are you two...all right? Something...happened, didn't it?" Aiz finally asked, concern tinting her voice as she surveyed the two in front of her.

"Indeed," Lefiya started, fully prepared to explain the eye-opening experience, when suddenly—

"Riveria! Over here!"

"Little Argonaut's here, too!"

—two Amazonian voices called out as Tione and Tiona dropped onto the ground nearby, the same as Aiz had done moments earlier. The three elites now gathered, Lefiya began to relay everything that had happened, as well as her conjectures—though only after they were out of Bell's earshot, of course.

By the time Riveria showed up, she'd already finished her story, Aiz, Tiona, and Tione all sporting curious expressions as they mulled over the situation in their minds.

"…Thanks for filling us in. Riveria and the rest of us will stay here and investigate a bit. Aiz, you take these two back to camp for now."

"But…but Miss Tione, I—?!" Lefiya started, feeling very much as though she, having witnessed everything directly, should be part of the investigation.

Tione, however, stopped her short. "You're to do as you're told, Lefiya. Besides, you're the only one capable of explaining the situation to everyone back at camp. Right, Riveria?"

"Quite right. Depending on how things play out, Finn may need to rally the rest of the party. The faster we can fill him in, the better," Riveria concurred, making her way toward the group with long silver staff in hand.

"Oh…" Lefiya let her voice fall, knowing she'd been soundly beaten.

Tiona beamed at the elf, her own Urga primed and ready in her arms. "You guys look beat! Get some rest, yeah? No need to push yourselves!" And then, "Little Argonaut especially."

Surprised, Lefiya turned around to see Bell standing a short distance away. While his wounds had been fully healed, he looked, indeed, just as tired as Tiona had suggested. The final blow, so to speak, that neither healing magic nor potions could mend, was the fatigue left over from battle—a fatigue now peeking through the strong front he was attempting to maintain.

To up and leave him now, after being the one to get him into this mess, would simply be cruel—not from a perspective of reasonableness but simply from her as an elf.

A feeling of awkwardness creeping up under her collar, she obediently nodded. "…All right."

"Take care of them, Aiz," Riveria said as she handed Aiz her portable magic-stone lantern.

"Of course."

Then, Tiona and the others throwing them a wave, they said their short good-byes and began the trek back to camp.

"…You're sure you're all right?" Aiz asked once the three had made it a short way into the dark woods, worry coloring her voice.

"Ah-ha-ha…I-I'm fine! Really. Already got healed and everything, yeah?" Bell forced a laugh, his energy nothing but a facade as he let his gaze wander down by his feet.

"But your shoes, they're…awful…" Aiz shone the lantern in the direction of said boots, so ragged at this point that they scarcely resembled foot attire.

In fact, both Lefiya's and Bell's battle clothes were littered with rips and holes where the acid had melted them away, but their shoes were, by far, the worst victims, having been submerged so long in the acid. Until the masked adventurer's ministrations, the skin beneath them, too, had been equally as torn up, but now they simply looked as though a great many moths had eaten away at them.

"I have a set of greaves back at camp…" Bell murmured.

Lefiya shot him a sidelong glance before asserting herself none too subtly. "I'll give you a new pair of boots once we get back. If I'm unable to find any, I'll buy you some from Rivira."

"R-really? I-I mean…are you sure?"

"Of course I am," she replied equally as bluntly as he whirled around to look at her. "Don't…don't misunderstand me. I simply… feel as though I need to make up for involving you in this entire affair. That's it!" She hissed the last part through gritted teeth.

Bell blinked once, twice, then gave her a somewhat awkward, somewhat sheepish grin.

Lefiya, in turn, jerked her head away with a harrumph, attempting to disguise her own embarrassment.

"…"

Aiz stared at them in silence, jaw slack.

"You two…are getting along now?"

"What?!" Lefiya practically screamed, whirling around. "Y-you have it all wrong, Miss Aiz! Truly! T-to think something like that would ever happen in the history of the entire world would… would…!"

"Ha-ha-ha…" Bell laughed, a smile rising to his face.

"Yooooooooooooooooou! Stop that right now! Tell her! Tell Miss Aiz that she is utterly incorrect in her assumption!!"

"Yep, you're getting along now…"

"No, it's—Miss Aiz! Listen to meeeeeeeeeeeeeeeeeeeeee!!"

But Lefiya could only wail in vain as Bell feigned laughter at her beloved swordswoman's entirely off-base observation, the swordswoman herself nodding in her own self-directed affirmation.

Far up above them, the crystalline night sky glittered as it watched over their return.

FLIP SIDE OF THE STAGE

Гэта казка іншага сям'і.

За кулісамі

The crystals growing from the Dungeon floor glimmered with a hazy, surreal blue glow.

Deep, deep in the forest, they shed their light at the floor's easternmost tip.

And from within those mighty crystals, towering among the trees, a cry of anguish reverberated against their glistening surfaces.

There were two of them, gasping for breath. Above them, a figure stood with small *tachi* unsheathed, shrouded in darkness as their long cape fluttered in a nonexistent breeze.

Blood dripped from the silver blade's gleaming edge.

"Now then, there are a few things I'd like to ask the both of you," the adventurer began in a low voice, her face hidden deep within her hood as she looked down upon the two figures on the ground.

The two men were currently lying crumpled at her feet.

It was the same two Evils associates who had sicced the swarm of violas on Lefiya and Bell earlier.

The young human and elf, now laid bare of their forehead protectors and hoods, trembled with fear as the cerulean eyes of the masked adventurer cut into them with an icy glare.

"Were you the ones who released that monster here? And if so, what are you trying to attain?" The girl's voice was cold, calculating, entirely unbefitting the adventurer who'd only a short while ago been healing her fellow elf and white-haired companion.

Bright-red splatters of blood dotted the surrounding greenery. Her weapon had cut them down to the bone, slicing through muscle and sinew and rendering them incapable of movement.

She'd gone after them the moment she'd left Lefiya and Bell, mostly due to her concern regarding the new monster species she'd fought earlier but also due to the twinge of doubt she just couldn't shake off.

This grand forest was like her playground, after all.

She knew where the white flowers grew, flowers she offered to the graves of her fallen comrades. She even knew where the wild fruit grew. She knew the forest so well, in fact, that the moment she'd given chase after the two men below her, their fate had already been sealed.

"Gwahh…!" the man on the ground groaned, his robes wide open to reveal the countless crimson pellets lining his body—firestones, to be used for his own self-destruction.

Neither one of them had been granted poison capsules in their teeth. Even if they were to attempt to cut their own lives short, the only way out was fire—otherwise, the hieroglyphics on their backs, the Falna that would reveal both their true names and the name of their patron deity, could be revealed with a Status Thief.

Knowing all this, the masked adventurer made no attempt to stuff their mouths.

She held their lives—and their deaths—firmly in the grip of her hand, words callous as they hissed between her teeth. "I've seen these…self-immolation tools of yours before." Her eyes narrowed, voice lowering further still. "They stole the lives of one of my comrades," she spit out. "You're survivors of *that*…familia, then? The 'Evils,' as they call themselves?"

The air ran thick with her hatred.

Down on the ground, the two men could do nothing but tremble, the elf's pure, unadulterated contempt pressing down on them from all sides.

They cowered like frightened rats, sweat pouring off them in rivers, and the thickset human, at least, seemed to have lost control of his bowels.

"If you don't start talking, I'll have to defile those backs of yours. And if I find you're colluding with some kind of nefarious deity, I'll have no choice but to wipe you off the face of this earth."

"P-please, no! I-I'm begging you!!" the human suddenly screamed, no longer able to hold it in. He desperately attempted to put distance between himself and the demon in elf's clothing staring murderously down at him, but she quickly put a stop to his retreat.

The male elf, on the other hand…simply watched his companion struggle and writhe with a tight-lipped laugh.

"Ha-ha…ha-ha-ha…"

"Is something funny?"

"Y-your eyes. I can tell from your eyes. You seek revenge…and you won't stop until you've achieved it." Another laugh. "You're just like me."

It was a laugh of scorn. Of pity. And as the masked adventurer looked down at the elf and his derisive gaze, her eyes narrowed to slits.

"Nameless kin of mine, do you not, too, wish to lay your eyes once more upon those whom you've loved…those whom you've lost to the cruel reality of death?"

"You cannot bring back the dead."

"And yet such a meeting exists within the realms of possibility."

"What are you talking about?"

The elf continued to laugh, his gleeful snickering forming a network of creases in the girl's brow. His human companion, on the other hand, remained crouched in terror, staring at the elf with a look of sheer disbelief.

Perhaps he took pity on her—an elf like himself, with a similar history. Whatever the reason, he continued in a tremulous whisper as he spoke of the unspeakable.

"Swear your allegiance to our master. Then you, too, shall—"

Suddenly—

—a brilliant flash of silver light shot toward them from straight overhead.

In a show of breathtaking quickness, the masked adventurer leaped out of the way, dodging the attack meant for her. The same could not be said for the two men, however, the knives plunging deep into their necks.

"Ghu…ah…?"

"Wha?"

The girl's eyes widened as blood sprayed from their lips.

One after another, the dark projectiles came hurtling through the air. Quickly distancing herself from the two men, she waited and watched for the second wave that was sure to come.

She watched for a further moment as blood gurgled out from the fresh holes in the men's necks—they wouldn't be telling her anything else, that was for sure—then checked behind her to see the source of the incoming blades.

Her eyes caught sight of a hooded purplish-blue robe among the rustling upper branches.

But she couldn't identify its owner, a strangely patterned mask obscuring the figure's face.

"Evils scum…Nothing but incompetent fools keen on making nuisances of themselves."

The voice from beneath its mask was spine-tingingly disquieting, almost as though multiple people were speaking at the same time.

One metal-gloved hand disappeared into the robes before reemerging with a brilliant red magic sword.

"—"

All of a sudden, time slowed down to a crawl.

The figure's sword moved. It was so fast, she could barely see it let alone react to it.

The glowing ball of flames it launched swallowed up the two Evils associates, dying breaths and all.

"Gnngh—?!"

She leaped back just in time, cape fluttering, before the resulting explosion lit up the sky.

The fireball had set off the firestones lining the two men's robes.

Barely managing to escape the blast zone, she stood back and scrutinized the scene of carnage in front of her. The gouged earth; the blazing grasses; and the charred, shredded bodies of the two men in its midst. All around her, the nauseating stench of burned flesh saturated the air.

She looked toward the branches above, but the masked figure was already gone.

"…"

So much for getting any information. Her one source had been effectively snuffed out.

They got me good, she thought with frustration.

A sigh passing her lips, she quickly scanned the perimeter. Fortunately, the massive crystals surrounding the area were keeping the flames fairly well contained, stopping the fire from spreading farther into the forest. She made her way toward the center of the blast, smoke and embers whirling around her.

It would be of no use to search the men's bodies. The firestones had done their job well—one could barely tell the flaming remains were even human. Various body parts lay strewn about, crackling and smoking and entirely unrecognizable.

With one last pitying glance, she prepared to make herself scarce.

"...?"

Until a sudden glint stopped her in her tracks.

Walking over to a nearby bit of brush, she stooped down to pick up the source of the tiny light.

"What's this...?"

It had belonged to the two men, no doubt. Though that would mean it was considerably resilient. Had it been tossed over here during the explosion?

Bits of it were, indeed, charred, but its general shape and structure remained intact.

It was an ingot of human construction, big enough to rest comfortably in her palm.

A strange red orb, like an eye, almost, was inlaid within its body, and what appeared to be a letter *D* had been carved into its surface, resembling neither Koine script nor the hieroglyphics of the gods.

"...Some kind of magic item?" she murmured to herself, voice heavy with doubt.

Then, tucking the stone away inside her robes, she disappeared into the night.

"We couldn't find anything, Lefiya."

Finn spoke as the white crystalline light of "morning" shone down across the eighteenth floor. Most of *Loki Familia*'s members were scouring the forest in search of clues when he approached the young mage, his words earning him a look of bewilderment.

"But that's..."

It had been less than twenty-four hours since their battle in that pit.

Upon Lefiya's relay of the events, Finn had ordered a large-scale search of the eastern part of the forest. He'd had faith in her theory—that the two Evils associates must have been protecting something, hiding something, if it justified going so far as to install that trap monster, the "Guardian of the Forest."

And yet, the results were just as Finn had said.

No matter how much they combed the massive forest in increasingly larger circles, they discovered absolutely nothing—not a stone out of place nor a trace of questionable goings-on.

Lefiya, now recovered after a night's rest, could only look out across the surrounding forest and at her weary companions in confusion.

"B-but...but Captain, we...we truly did fight for our lives against that brightly colored monster!"

"I'm not saying that I don't believe you. I actually believe your theory is correct. You don't need to produce the hole itself for you to persuade me," the prum commander responded as he surveyed the ground in front of them, where traces of Lefiya's and Bell's magic scarred the land. The mess made it look almost as if the very stone itself had split and crumbled.

All around them, large pieces of crystal lay scattered about, broken off from their toppled pillars. Already, however, new crystal columns were poking out of the ground to take their place, the stone circle regenerating itself. It would seem the Dungeon's restorative properties were especially swift in this region.

Finn narrowed his pool-like green eyes, long Durandal spear in hand. "There was something here...and perhaps it yet remains."

"..."

"If it's the latter, however, it's not anything we'll be able to find as we are now." Finn gave his thumb a lick, muttering in self-assurance. "Regardless, it wouldn't do us any good to continue our search. That's my guess, anyway."

"Then we're just going to…?"

"Yes, it's time we put this place behind us. Gareth and the others back at camp will undoubtedly have finished packing, as well."

Riveria, Gareth, Aiz, and the rest of the party were currently back at the base camp, readying the group for their return to the surface.

Everyone was tired. There had been far too many incidents already on this expedition, and they weren't about to miss their day of departure.

It was crucial that they meet with Loki and relay everything they'd learned.

Lefiya had no choice but to hold her tongue at Finn's decision.

"Still, I can't deny the very distinct stench permeating this place. We'll be back to investigate again once we've gotten everything in order."

"…Understood, sir…"

"Then we head out. Raul! Let's bring it in! Call everyone back!"

"Roger that!"

The scattered members of the search party began to make their way back toward Finn.

Lefiya could only stare at the remains of the hole where she'd fought the trap monster, staff gripped tightly in her hands.

Knowing nothing of the masked adventurer's meeting with the two Evils associates, *Loki Familia* left the eastern edge of the forest behind them.

EPILOGUE

HOMEWARD
BOUND

Гэта казка іншага сям'і.

Вярнуць на месца

"What the hell is all this about that rabbit brat bein' here, huh? Why does no one tell me anything?!"

"'Cause we knew you'd throw a fit, just like you're doin' now! Come on, already! Get ready to go!"

"I'll show you a fit, you stupid Amazon!"

The day had finally arrived for *Loki Familia*'s expedition party to return to the surface.

And the camp was already abuzz with morning activity.

Everyone was preparing for the departure. All around Aiz, her companions were folding up their tents and packing everything away in large cargo bins for easy transport. It had been in the midst of all this bustling activity that Bete had first been made aware of Bell's presence in the camp, a fact he didn't take to calmly, and about which he was currently interrogating Tiona and Tione.

Indeed, given the werewolf's recent trip up to the surface, everything that had happened with Bell would come as a great surprise. Even last night, when Bete had finally returned, he'd been too tired to even notice the additional guests they'd picked up, having gone straight into the nearest tent and promptly passed out.

Tiona and Tione had known all too well what effect the news would have on Bete, so they'd done what they always did and simply told him nothing.

"Hey! Aiz! Is it true? About the rabbit brat?" Bete turned toward Aiz, clearly not trusting anything the two Amazonian sisters might have told him, as a very obvious vein started to bulge atop his forehead.

"It's…true, yes," she responded frankly, nodding.

"The hell!" Bete stuck out his tongue in disgust…before slowly clamping his mouth shut.

All of a sudden, a very strange, awkward silence washed over him.

Aiz cocked her head to the side in confusion before Bete leaned forward, his voice no more than a hissed whisper.

"Th-then…then is it true?"

"Is what true…?"

"You know. *That!* That, uh…you know…about him peekin' in on all you girls durin' a bath!"

And here the Sword Princess Protection Unit had sworn everyone to secrecy! The normally impassive Aiz felt a flush rise to her cheeks as her eyes widened in surprise.

Her gaze dropped to her feet as she began rubbing her hands together, the same way she had last night, before finally, not saying a word, she nodded. There was no way to hide her embarrassment.

Bete stopped short in shock upon the confirmation of his fears.

"That…that bastard! So easily accomplishing what I never could!" His entire body trembled with unadulterated rage at the (albeit misunderstood) image in his head.

"…Aiz."

Just as Aiz was about to explain that Hermes had lured Bell in, Bete pulled an about-face, suddenly impossible to read, almost as though his earlier outburst had never happened.

His amber eyes stared at her with a kind of wild glint.

"If he made it here…to the middle levels…then that means he's a Level Two now?"

Aiz nodded a second time.

"That bastard…" Bete repeated with a curse. "Where is he, huh?"

"…"

It was the question she'd been dreading.

Aiz's expression hardened—looking not altogether dissimilar to her normal expression—as her mouth clamped shut.

Where was Bell? In his tent, no doubt. She'd seen him and Hestia slip inside there not more than a short while ago.

But Aiz wasn't about to tell Bete this. In fact, Aiz was hoping to keep Bell and Bete from meeting altogether.

It had happened almost two weeks ago now—on the first day of their expedition. They'd been winding through the seventh floor when, for whatever reason, Aiz had incurred the greatest shock of all time—the realization that the goal Bell aspired to might be none other than Bete. Even now, she hadn't quite been able to shake away this thought. And though she'd had many chances to ask him about it now, she'd gotten cold feet every time.

What if it was true, and it was actually Bete who was spurring the boy on?

—Mister Bete! All of this has been for you! I'd do anything for you to accept me!

—Haaah? You really think I give a rat's ass about any of that?!

The scene played out in Aiz's mind like some kind of romantic comedy, glittering eyes and all.

…She didn't like that.

No, she didn't like it one single bit.

In fact, Little Aiz inside her was currently balled up with her arms around her knees as she pouted in silence.

She didn't want to see that. It was far too heartrending.

Which was why, in that moment, Aiz simply decided to play dumb.

"………………Over there somewhere," she responded in what could only be referred to as a bald-faced lie, avoiding eye contact with Bete as she pointed in the completely wrong direction.

"Over here, huh?" Bete repeated to himself as he took off in said direction, clearly ready to pick a bone with someone.

It pained Aiz greatly to lie, but even despite the guilt tugging at the back of her mind, she'd have done the same thing over again if given the choice. Come to think of it, even Bete's typical name for the boy had leveled up—no longer "tomato brat" but "rabbit brat." Yes, she'd done the right thing, she thought to herself, gulping inwardly.

"…Hey. I need to fix up my friends' weapons. Gimme a whetstone and some tools, would ya?"

"Hmph! Is that how you talk to someone when you're askin' for a favor, Welfy?"

"…Could I please…borrow some tools?"

© Kiyotaka Haimura

"Whazzat? I didn't heeeeeaaaaar you!"

"Damn you...!!"

All around her, preparations were reaching a climax. As lower-level members rushed back and forth wildly finishing things up, Tsubaki had her own hands full making life difficult for a certain young smith in the middle of the camp. It had been decided that the group would be split into two, and Tsubaki and the rest of *Hephaistos Familia*, along with Bell and his party, would be the second party to depart.

The vanguard, which would include Aiz, was already leaving the campsite behind—they were on their way to the south, toward the passageway that led to the next floor up. Others in Aiz's group included Finn and Lefiya (already having returned from their search in the eastern forest), as well as Tiona, Tione, and the other elites, since they would need ample fighting power if they were to take down the seventeenth floor's Monster Rex, Goliath—which Bete had successfully slipped by during his earlier antivenin run. Speaking of Bete, he, too, had (begrudgingly) joined the advanced group, never locating Bell after Aiz's deception.

It was time to go.

She had everything equipped, from her breastplate to her waist guard. Trusted sword by her side, Aiz made her way to where Tiona and the others awaited, and from there, the party began their trek to the cave that would lead them to the next floor.

"M-Miss Aiz!"

When suddenly...

...a voice called out from behind her.

She could identify him from his voice alone, her eyes widening in soft surprise as she turned around from her spot at the back of the line.

The white-haired boy in question hesitated a moment before making his way toward her.

"You're...going already?"

"Yes...I'm part of the advance party, after all."

Bell was also decked out in his lightweight armor, readying himself for their return to the Dungeon proper.

He looked good. Recovered. The dark shadow of fatigue was gone from his eyes and face, and the energy was back in his arms and legs.

Aiz felt relief wash through her. Only then.

"I-I, uh…"

"?"

Bell's eyes shifted back and forth as if he had something he wanted to say.

He looked doleful almost…and Aiz could only blink curiously as he struggled with whatever complex mixture of emotions was pulling at his thoughts.

Finally, however, his gaze rose, the turmoil gone from his eyes.

"Please…be careful."

Shock washed over her like a tidal wave.

They were words the Sword Princess hadn't heard in a long, long time, even from her own companions in *Loki Familia*.

While this was only proof that those around her had nothing but faith in her and her strength, there was something about hearing them now, after so long, that made her heart warm with affection.

"…You…be careful, too."

Her lips had unknowingly turned into a soft smile.

"I'll see you later."

"…"

And with that, Aiz turned away, leaving the boy behind her.

It was actually very possible that they wouldn't see each other again upon their return to the surface. Aiz would go back to her home, and Bell would go back to his.

When would their next meeting be?

It was this question that plagued Aiz's mind as she walked away, her parting words still hanging in the air.

"What were you 'n' Little Argonaut talkin' about, hmmm, Aiz?"

"Just…good-byes."

"You're sure you didn't ask him how he got all his abilities to S?

Sure would've been nice if you had. I mean, if he was gonna tell anyone, it'd definitely be you!"

"I…don't think that would work…"

Tiona and the others were as talkative as ever as they made their way through the forest.

Laughing along at their antics, Aiz glanced to where Lefiya was walking alongside her.

"Did you say your good-byes, Lefiya?" she asked, still under the assumption that the two had completely patched up their relationship.

"…" The elf's face turned sour. "…I've already said everything I needed to say."

"?"

I'm sorry. Thank you. But I still don't forgive you.

Those were the three things she'd expressed last night. Was that really everything she had to say?

Aiz could only cock her head to the side in curiosity at the young elf's expression, Tiona and the others still chatting idly about the boy behind her.

"All right, then. There's something I'd like to confirm before we head to the seventeenth floor." Finn brought the group to a stop once they were clear of the forest, gathered together in front of the cave along the southern wall.

He would be leading the vanguard on their trek to the surface, and Riveria and Gareth would do the same for the squad that would follow soon after. Scanning the group, his eyes passed from Tiona, Tione, Bete, Lefiya, and Aiz to the faces of Raul and the other lower-level *Loki Familia* members.

"The floor boss Goliath lurks in the hall above us. We will, of course, eliminate him. Normally, this would be a great opportunity for everyone, not just the elites, to gain some experience…However, these are no ordinary circumstances, and we're still hurting greatly from encountering a string of Irregulars during our expedition. For this reason, I would like Aiz and the others to participate in the battle from the beginning. I don't imagine…anyone will be against this, yes? All of us are quite anxious to see the sun again.

And truthfully, even I'm itching to crawl back into my own bed for a good night's sleep."

The group erupted in laughter and smiles at the small captain's words of jest.

"Why not sleep together with me!" Tione called out, completely misreading the moment and being held back only by her sister, draining the tension from the faces and shoulders of Raul and the others.

Finn waited for a moment before straightening out his expression.

"Tiona, Tione, Bete—you three will be on the front line. While I won't say anything if you bring Goliath down entirely, focus first on simply containing him. Whatever you do, keep that magic stone of his under control."

"Ooooookaaaaay!"

"Understood, sir!"

"Got it."

"Aiz, you're in the center. You'll act as backup wherever it's needed, offense or defense," Finn continued.

"Understood."

"Raul, you and the other lower-level members will guard the back line. It'll be your job to ensure that any overflow from that wall takes care of the surrounding monsters."

"Roger!"

"Mages, begin casting the moment we enter the main hall. Once you're ready, launch all you have at once. That should eliminate everything, Goliath included. You'll give the signal, Lefiya."

"I-I will?!"

Finn relayed his orders in turn.

He was calm, with a sort of all-knowing air, as though he didn't even have to think about it.

"It should be over in three minutes. Let's go—everyone, prepare for battle!"

Every hand readied a weapon in one coordinated movement.

They were ready—Orario's top elites—and the only ones capable of taking down a Monster Rex in a matter of minutes.

Aiz let her eyes travel upward, peering into the darkness of the dim tunnel before them.

Grruuuuaaaaaaaaaooooooogh!!—Then they ran, the roar of the mighty beast beckoning them into its lair.

" ... "

The torchlights flickered.

Darkness saturated the stone room, its construction not altogether unlike the ancient shrines of old, and it was silent save for the crackling of flame. They were in the Chamber of Prayers beneath Orario's Guild Headquarters.

The venerable god Ouranos narrowed his brine-colored eyes from atop the throne at the room's center, four torches illuminating him from every side.

"What is it, Ouranos?" The black-robed figure next to him spoke up as the aged god stared down at his feet.

"My voice no longer reaches the Dungeon," Ouranos replied to the Magus Fels's question.

Fels stiffened, jet-black robes shuddering from the sudden shout. "You don't mean...the prayers have been cut off?!"

"Indeed. The Dungeon is...unstable," Ouranos responded, visibly rattled. His eyes bored grimly into the floor below, toward the winding labyrinth under his feet. "I can only guess that another god has entered its halls, and the Dungeon has taken notice. Yet that would mean..." he began, motionless, before letting his own thought die.

A heavy silence weighed down on him, suffocating, almost as though the fears gripping his heart were simply too much to bear.

"Ouranos...could this mean...?"

"Yes..." The old god nodded. "With Zeus gone, it seems to be... mutating." He turned his eyes toward the ceiling, shrouded in darkness, his gaze somewhere far, far away.

Then, finally, his eyelids fell in silence.

"...?"

A tremor underfoot caught Aiz's attention, and she turned her gaze groundward.

"A quake...?"

"The Dungeon, is it...shaking?"

Soon, the entire vanguard—Tiona, Tione, Bete, Lefiya, and the others—was staring at their feet.

They'd made it to the Dungeon's upper levels, the eighth floor.

Already free of the middle levels and feeling decidedly less tense as a result, they felt the sudden trembling of the earth below them, and it brought the group to a halt. Anything unexpected could be the harbinger of an Irregular, after all. As first-tier adventurers, they knew this well.

Even the monsters roaming about the floor scuttled away in fear.

Startled and confused, they could only throw one another looks of abject concern at the quake seemingly who knew how many floors beneath their feet.

"Captain..." Raul's voice trembled slightly.

"...We keep moving. Reaching the surface is our top priority. Cruz, take Narfi, then go make sure Riveria and the others behind us are fine—just in case," Finn responded calmly, in direct contrast to Raul's open unease. The chienthrope Cruz nodded with a quick "Understood" before grabbing Narfi and heading back along the main route.

The rest of the group, as per Finn's instructions, pushed ahead as planned.

They made it all the way to the Dungeon entrance, in fact, as the rumblings stopped almost as quickly as they'd started.

The party made their way up the great spiral steps and exited the enormous hole in the ground, emerging from Babel's gate.

The breeze tickled their skin.

It was the surface.

"Ahhhhh, how I've missed this!!" Tiona exhaled in a grand show of emotion, still holding her Urga.

And, indeed, the warm sunlight, great blue sky, and rejuvenating breeze were enough to bring smiles to every face in *Loki Familia*'s expedition vanguard.

"The sun is setting..." Lefiya murmured, eyes unexpectedly wet with tears.

"It's always so bright stepping out after an expedition," Tione commented, squinting, unaccustomed to the light.

Before them, the city's Central Park was awash in brilliant red crimson.

To the west, the sun was gradually sinking beneath the city's walls.

It was a sight they'd seen so many times already, and yet at that moment, after having fought for their lives deep within the earth, it was the most beautiful thing they'd ever laid eyes upon, more precious than the most valuable of treasures.

They waited there for the rest of the group. It took about thirty minutes, the crew gathering considerable attention in their spot along the northern edge of the park, but finally, the other party appeared with Gareth and Riveria in the lead, carting large cargo packs laden with their equipment and items.

They broke into smiles as quickly as Tiona and the others had as they took in great gulps of fresh surface air.

"Those kids...they're still on the eighteenth floor?" Aiz asked of Riveria as the two groups converged, free from casualties.

"Yes. It would seem they had some sort of minor business to attend to."

While Aiz couldn't help the worry that bubbled to the surface of her mind, she followed her companions home all the same.

"Well, that sure was fun! You folks get into any other business downstairs, you gimme a call, okay?"

"Thank you, Tsubaki."

The two familias, sworn to Loki and Hephaistos, went their separate ways in the park.

Tsubaki and Finn, the former with her uncovered eye crinkling in mirth and the latter with a smile on his face, shook hands upon their parting, prompting the rest of their familias to do the same. The adventurers shook hands and knocked shoulders with the smiths.

Finally, the craftsmen and their hammers took their leave, and the two familias walked in opposite directions and back to their respective homes. First, out of Central Park, then down North Main Street, and finally, into the complex series of side streets and roads that would lead them home.

As the group lugged their heavy bags along in triumphant return, they were met with a grand welcome, the citizens of Orario offering them greetings and blessings from the sides of the street or the upper windows of their homes. The welcoming cheers of adults and adoring gazes of children were enough to instill a sort of pride within *Loki Familia*'s hearts, as well as the tiniest glimmer of embarrassment, as they made their way along the crimson, sun-drenched street.

It wasn't long before the overlapping towers of their home appeared before them.

"We made it…" Tiona murmured beneath her breath.

It was a grand mansion, sitting along a winding road away from the main street to the north of town.

It stretched higher and wider than any of its surrounding buildings.

The members of *Loki Familia* all took a moment to look up at their home, Twilight Manor.

"We've returned. Open the gate," Finn instructed the guards at the manor's entrance, who responded respectfully with a pair of broad smiles.

Already, their numerous companions who'd stayed behind were cramming themselves into the narrow corridor just inside the gate.

Suddenly—

"Welcome baaaaaaaaaaaaaaaaaaaaaaaaaaaaaack!!"

—a shadow raced forth from the mansion to greet them, almost as though she'd been lying in wait.

The crimson-haired goddess bolted straight past the men, not stopping until she'd reached Aiz and the other women.

And then, she leaped.

"How are ya?! Everyone okay? I'm so excited that you're back! Ahhhhhhhh!" The womanizing goddess flew at them with her arms outstretched, same as always. First Aiz, then Tiona, then Tione quickly sidestepped her wriggling reach, same as always.

And, same as always, Lefiya alone was left at the end of the line—

"I...*P-please don't!!*"

"Gwuuaagh?!"

Grabbing the incoming hands by the wrists, Lefiya threw Loki to the floor beside her.

Aiz and the other girls exchanged looks of admiration, applauding the elf's magnificent performance.

"Gnnmph...You've...gotten stronger, Lefiya. Barely recognize ya..." Loki groaned as she writhed on the ground, beaming with approval despite the tears stinging her eyes.

"Please refrain from such perverse behavior!" the panting, red-faced elf shouted in response.

"We've returned with no casualties, Loki, and made some great gains. We have much to talk about...but perhaps you'd like to compose yourself first?" Finn approached with a smile.

Loki looked up at the prum from her spot on the ground before responding with a laugh of her own.

"Heh, ya make a good point! Right, then—first things first!" she proclaimed, springing to her feet before making a mad dash toward the manor.

She screeched to a halt in front of the other familia members who'd come out to greet the expedition party, then turned around to face them once more.

"We've got a real mess of problems on our side, but for the time bein'..."

Her eyes passed each of them in turn—Finn, Riveria, Gareth, Tiona, Tione, Bete, Lefiya, Raul and the other supporters, and finally, Aiz.

After she'd rounded the entire circle, her face broke out into a grin.

"Welcome home, everyone."

Everyone behind her raised their hands in a simultaneous cheer.

Their family was welcoming them back, and the sight brought smiles to the whole party.

"We're home."

Far above them atop the central tower, the Trickster flag fluttered in the breeze, glittering with a crimson radiance.

Loki Familia's long expedition had finally come to an end.

Bete · Loga

BELONGS TO:	Loki Familia		
RACE:	werewolf	JOB:	adventurer
DUNGEON RANGE:	fifty-ninth floor	WEAPONS:	metal boots, twin blades
CURRENT WORTH:	-47,800,000 valis		

Status   Lv.5

STRENGTH:	B 766	ENDURANCE:	C 647
DEXTERITY:	B 729	AGILITY:	S 965
MAGIC:	I 0	HUNTER:	G
IMMUNITY:	G	PUMMEL:	G
HEALING POWER:	H		

MAGIC:	Hati	• Enchant spell. • Fire Attribute. • Magic Drain. • Damage Drain.
SKILLS:	Úlfheðinn	• Can be activated only in moonlight. • Transforms into a werewolf. All abilities greatly increased. • Abnormal statuses neutralized.
SKILLS:	Fenris Wolf	• Increases running speed.
SKILLS:	Solmani	• Increases agility and strength when accelerating.

EQUIPMENT: Frosvirt

- Mythril metal boots.
- Crafted by *Hephaistos Familia*'s Tsubaki Collbrande for 93,000,000 valis.
- A custom-made order and an invention of Bete himself. The only Superior-grade weapon in Orario currently capable of draining magic.
- Already on the second iteration. Compared to the previous experimental version, this pair, reconstructed by Tsubaki after she got the hang of its composition, boasts considerably higher performance, making it a first-class weapon.

EQUIPMENT: Dual Roland

- Durandal.
- One of the "Roland Series" weapons crafted by master smith Tsubaki.
- Twin blades. Although they are Durandal weapons their low attack power is more in line with second-tier weapons.
- 108,000,000 valis.

BETE LOGA

© Kiyotaka Haimura

Afterword

I kept my page count in check while writing this volume so as not to repeat the same mistake I made on Volume 8 of the main series, which ended up making this fifth volume of the side series considerably shorter than its brothers. At any rate, I was able to finish it without any problems.

Chronologically, I was able to make this book match up with the main series (though a bit of book four worked its way in there, as well). Once again, I've been able to throw my characters from this side series together with my characters from the main series, this time in a sort of R and R episode.

To be quite honest, I didn't go into this book planning to reveal everything that was going on behind the scenes in the main series. Mostly I was just hoping to continue my original plot for this series, and I ended up having to write and rewrite parts of this volume to ensure nothing was inconsistent with the main books. Still, whenever a spot jumped out at me just begging for a bit of riposte, well… you can be assured I was nothing but smiles as I went with it.

I tried to be conscious of the events that took place in the previous book, but some of my more minor characters kept popping up with their own subplots, too. As I got to work with a large familia different from that of the main series, I really wanted to take advantage of and dig into the different relationships among all these characters. Seeing the unsung heroes getting their chance to shine, or even just doing something as simple as cooking a meal, is actually quite fun for me. That being said, I couldn't let them steal the show from the main characters, either.

So long as we're on the topic of side characters, the new manga version of *Sword Oratoria*, written by Takashi Yagi and currently being serialized by *GanGan Joker*, has a number of characters of its own who have been reimported into the series (with my permission, of course!). You may have a bit of fun comparing the two side by side in search of these hidden gems.

And on that note, let me segue into my thank-yous for this volume.

I'll start off with Takashi Yagi, who's turning my words into a wonderful series of pictures in the manga version of my series, which is something sure to make any author pleased as punch—thank you. I was more than happy to consent to your reimportation of those aforementioned scenes and characters. Then, of course, my editors, Otaki and Takahashi, as well as my illustrator, Kiyotaka Haimura, who once again colored my book with his fantastic illustrations. I'd also like to thank my dear Akamitsu Awamura, who gave me permission to use some of his ideas. I look forward to coming up with hilariously painful aliases together with you again.

And, of course, I'd like to express my utmost gratitude to you, my readers, who continue to read my poorly written blatherings.

Lately, I've begun receiving fan mail from some of you. I can't even begin to describe how happy it makes me to read them, so I just wanted to thank you from the depths of my heart. It seems I worried a number of people when I spoke of my recent weight loss in my afterword for book seven of the main series, but let me assure you that I'm now eating so much rice that I'm liable to die from it in order to get my weight back up. Your dear author is doing just fine. I'm sorry for upsetting you.

I'm thinking my next book will be a story focused on the Amazonian twins. I'll do my best to deliver it as soon as possible, so I hope you, too, will do your best to read it.

All the best.

Fujino Omori

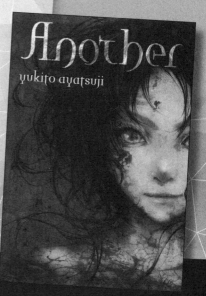

HE DOES NOT LET ANYONE ROLL THE DICE.

A young Priestess joins her first adventuring party, but blind to the dangers, they almost immediately find themselves in trouble. It's Goblin Slayer who comes to their rescue—a man who has dedicated his life to the extermination of all goblins by any means necessary. A dangerous, dirty, and thankless job, but he does it better than anyone. And when rumors of his feats begin to circulate, there's no telling who might come calling next...

Light Novel
V. 1-2
Available
Now!

Check out the simul-pub manga chapters every month!

Yen Press   YEN ON

www.yenpress.com

Goblin Slayer © Kumo Kagyu / Noboru Kannatuki / SB Creative Corp.